Sunrise Korea

By

Timo Annala

This book is a work of fiction. Places, events, and
situations in this story are purely fictional. Any resemblance
to actual persons, living or dead, is coincidental.

ISBN: 1-4107-0948-5 (e-book)
ISBN: 1-4107-0949-3 (Paperback)

This book is printed on acid free paper.

1stBooks - rev. 02/26/03

To those unwithering souls who seek justice before the Japanese Embassy in Seoul every Wednesday.

Prologue

Rain seared from the sky and stung like watery bullets. The wind swept the sea into rolling assaults that punished the coastline while lightning split from the dark heavens, making bright the night. Silver shards washed through the trees, over the lawn and into the castle whose proud brow looked over the cliff at the sea below. Its high turrets and many yellow eyes seemed filled with gold spilling out into the night as thunder fell upon it from the sky like a cascade of boulders. In the middle of the lawn, kneeling under the fury of the storm was a small guesthouse whose walls matched the castle's stony skin. Darkened windows peeked out from under a hood of rock. The next bolt lit two figures for a sliver of a second as they fled from the guesthouse towards the cliffs. The leading one was a woman, her mouth gaping while the wind tore her screams from her throat and threw them to where no one heard. The man behind her chased silently in his bare feet and black tuxedo, his eyebrows curled up in a scowl of malice and his lips pulled back before hungry teeth.

Part I

one

The plane seats were too stiff, too straight; she couldn't seem to find enough oxygen to breathe, and she was exhausted from the long flight. Most of all, she didn't want to talk anymore because the subject always made her deepest wounds tender again.

"And that's all I've ever known," Sumi sighed. Her hair framed her face like curtains of black silk while her eyes shone as coals from within. She propped her elbow on the armrest and leaned her head in her hand.

"So you never found out why she left Korea?" asked Greg, stroking her hair between his fingers. He leaned closer to her face in the sterile gloom of the plane's cabin.

"No," Sumi whispered back. "She refused to ever talk about it." A clear pearl began to swell at the bottom of her left eye. "She told me nothing of Korea, nothing of her parents or family, nothing at all of life before she came to L.A. And I've never known a single detail about my father, what he was like or how they met." Her lips tightened as she stared at the seat in front of her. "My mother was always such a stubborn woman."

Greg watched as the tear grew and burst over Sumi's eyelid, streaming down her left cheek, followed by an identical streak on the other side. He wiped her eyes softly and pulled her closer to his side. "She must have thought she was doing the best for you, protecting you from her past," he murmured. "Have you ever seen any old pictures of your family in Korea?"

"Just one. Mama always kept it by her bed. It was a black and white photo, but had faded a lot over the years." Sumi sniffed and turned to look out at the ocean below. "She's just a little girl in it, standing with her parents in front of a tiny house surrounded by fields. Oh, and I always remember staring at the small pony next to her, hitched up to a wagon."

"And you've never seen a picture of your dad?"

"Never."

"Well, hopefully this trip we'll show us more of your past. Remember, it was your mom's wish for us to come here, so maybe you'll finally find some answers."

"Maybe," she muttered, pressing her forehead against the plane's window. "But will I be able to accept what I find?"

Suddenly, a green tip of land appeared from under the plane's wing. "Look, Greg!" exclaimed Sumi, pulling on his arm. "We're here!"

Below, foamy lines of cotton separated the surrounding ocean blue from the dark coastline. Above the cliffs, deep green forests swept up the slopes and stood watch below the mountain's crown, an extinct volcano. Greg and Sumi watched as small towns sprouted amid the vegetation and black winding ribbons carried tiny cars and trucks over the island in slow motion.

Sumi felt her throat squeeze shut beneath her chin. Her fatigue had vanished like mist in the rising sun, and she could hardly believe the dreaminess of reality as she continued to watch the land slide by in silence. Within twisted claws of frozen lava, the volcanic island below held answers to her most searching questions about her past. Her journey here had begun when she was still a small child arriving home one afternoon and asking her mother where her father was. Some kids at school had wondered why she didn't have one and she was eager to find out. Many years and many more questions separated that girl and the woman in the window seat, and still she knew no more.

As far back as Sumi could remember, her mother had been a living secret. Any questions about their history had brought a swift and blinding response: "The past is lost! It's gone as though it never was. Place your care on the future, Sumi, and it will become what you wish it to be." She had learned not to inquire about life in Korea, or what it had been like for her mother to leave and settle in America. She had always assumed the reason for the silence lay buried with her father, somewhere in the shadowy mountains near the North Korean border.

The Korean War, along with all its evils, had separated her mother and her new groom at the threshold of their life together. Her father had been killed by a communist offensive north of Seoul, and her mother had fled to America not knowing she carried within her womb a budding baby girl.

This much, and not a breath more, had been told to Sumi about her earliest beginnings. No details about her father, no matter how much she begged, had ever left the barred heart and guarded lips of the wartime bride.

As the plane continued to descend, Sumi absorbed the landscape unfolding from beneath the steel wing. She saw jagged cliffs plunging vertically into a restless ocean, and trees clinging with rooted fingers to the island's edges, carpeting the wounded face of the rock beneath. While watching the island grow from the ocean, she realized she was seeing her mother's birthplace, what she had witnessed herself so many years past.

Sumi's thoughts bridged both the Pacific and the past to remember her ailing mother in that sterile hospital in Los Angeles just one year ago. She recalled the white walls and cream bedspread; she remembered the shiny chrome with the clear tubes; she could see her mother's shrunken face and weathered hands, and her timeless eyes. They had seen many dawns and dusks, and stormy nights too, and had witnessed atrocities that countries continued to debate and conceal to this day. Her hands, wrinkled and sun-soaked, had known the meaning of toil, and the futility of despair. Her mind had remained a sharpened blade, even while her armor had faded. And at the sunset of her struggles, as her last twilight surrounded her, she faced it with a strength that was able to mask the sickness which continued to leak her life away.

"Hi, my beauty. I was wondering when you'd be coming."

"Oh, Mama. I come everyday at this time. Any sooner and you complain because you miss your soaps," replied Sumi. Her soft lips and eyes smiled at her mother as she crossed the room to her bed. "How are you feeling today?"

"A little older and a little weaker. I'm not doing so well, Sumi dear," she answered. She sounded exhausted as her voice left her lips in cracked slices.

"Well, hopefully this helps. I brought you some of your favourite cucumber kimchi. I thought you might be craving it today. Greg should be coming by shortly to see you too." Sumi placed the plastic container on the table next to the bed, and pushed the grey hair of her mother's wig back from her face. She looked into her eyes and marveled at their brilliance and fire, still clear as ice after all these years. They shone like black pearls set in a pouch of dried leather as they smiled up at Sumi and were grateful.

"Thank you for the kimchi. It will be a wonderful switch after all this hospital food. Whatever taste it might have is robbed by these awful pills."

"I know, mom. I hate the pain you're going through."

"Love, we all must go through pain sometime, and some of us more than others." She coughed lightly. "But no regrets, Sumi. I have many wonderful memories, and I've had a very fortunate life. I am grateful for what I've been given. I hope you always strive to be grateful as well. It will carry you." She coughed again and held her hand to her chest.

"Mom, rest. Don't strain yourself," soothed Sumi, sliding her fingers along her mother's creased brow.

"I must, love," she wheezed. "I haven't long now."

A slim man appeared in the doorway. His face was tan and smooth as he smiled at the two women from the far side of the room.

"Sorry I'm late," he said as he reached Sumi's side. "Traffic's really snarling up out there. I got here as fast as I could." He pushed his black hair back from his face and squeezed Sumi's mother's hand. "How is the most wonderful mother-in-law in the world?"

"Not so great, Greg," she answered, chuckling. "Thanks for coming. Now that you're both here, I have something to tell you." She paused and painfully cleared her throat. "I have little time left, and less breath. My days are passing quickly." Her voice came in a hoarse whisper now. "I love you both and I have a final request to make."

"Mama, don't talk like that. You're still strong. You can beat this." Tears filled the floors of Sumi's eyes.

"I know, Sumi, I know. But if it's not this, it will be something else. We all have to go sometime. I'm just telling you this now in case I leave sooner rather than later." She took Sumi's hand in one of hers and Greg's in the other. "I want you to promise me something." Her unwavering eyes looked from Greg to Sumi.

"Sure, mom," answered Sumi.

"Of course, anything," Greg pledged.

"After I die, I want you to make a trip to Jeju Island. I want you to stay at the Sunrise Hotel, if it's still standing. That's where your father and I spent our honeymoon. I want you to know where you come from, Sumi."

"We'll certainly do that, won't we, Greg?" Sumi turned to her husband, her lips forming a thin line across her mouth.

"Absolutely," he replied.

"I know I've kept much of your past from you, my daughter. I wished to shield you so you wouldn't be burdened by it. I see now that it would be good for you to know your roots." She paused and put her hand on her chest while she drew several shallow breaths. "I want you to see it for yourself, to see your sunrise."

"I will, mom. We'll go." Sumi struggled to contain the well of tears rising to her eyes as she looked into her mother's dark pupils. Her face had never looked so frail and thin, but her words bothered Sumi far more.

"But that's enough of that. I'm not ready to leave just yet." She squeezed Greg and Sumi's hands tightly as she flashed them a brilliant smile. "Now you two better go. I know you have a special evening planned."

"That's not as important as you, mom."

"Go! I never wanted to be a burden on anyone and that hasn't changed. Don't worry about me, I'll be fine."

"Are you sure, Mama?" asked Sumi, unwilling to leave.

"I'm in a hospital, dear. I think I'll be all right. You two enjoy yourselves. It's only once a year, you deserve it." Still smiling, she pushed them away.

Sumi leaned over and kissed the weathered cheeks. "I love you, Mama."

"And I love you."

"Take care, Mrs. Park. I'll see you again soon," Greg said as he pulled the blanket higher and kissed her wrinkled hand.

"I'm sure you will," she returned, her smile fading on her lips.

Sumi had already left the room with Greg following when Mrs. Park called him back.

"Oh, just a second, Sumi," he called ahead to her down the hall. "Your mom needs me to fix her pillow behind her before we go. I'll meet you down at the car."

Sumi continued along the corridor to the elevators. She thought about what her mom had said, and how her eyes had seemed kinder at that moment than she had ever known them. She seemed to have told me more through her eyes than with her words, Sumi mused as she waited in front of the metallic doors. She looked down the empty hall, where the fluorescent ceiling lights stretched to an unseen end, and was about to turn back when the elevator doors hissed open.

9

Hesitating for a moment, she entered the elevator and pushed the main floor button, the 'M' burning with a crimson flame. Mama needs to rest and get some sleep right now, Sumi thought. She sounded so tired. I'll make sure to come a bit earlier tomorrow so we can spend more time together.

The steel doors slid closed.

Her mother never awoke again.

two

The plane skimmed over twisting shores that sent black arms of rock out into the ocean while sometimes, a cove of white sand would flash by, guarded on both sides by darkened lava. Sumi watched from her window and wondered what lay before her. The lush green hills below held many fears for her, and she was far from certain she wanted to know everything that had slept undisturbed down there for so long. Still, her heart dared to hope that this island of mysteries would match her questions with answers and finally grant her peace.

"I'm so tired," she sighed, leaning back in her seat and rubbing her eyes.

Greg reached over and took her hand in his. "Don't worry, we'll soon be down there," he said, continuing to marvel at the ragged shoreline looming nearer. "I'll be glad to be on the ground again, too."

The captain's droning broadcast, made in both Korean and English, announced the final approach into Jeju. The large plane steadied itself against the crosswind and leveled out as it roared over the harbour thronged with fishing boats and the city streets choked with cars.

Sumi turned from the window and looked into her husband's tired face. His warm smile lit her own and helped stuff her creeping fears a little lower in her chest. "Thanks for being here with me, Greg," she murmured. Though she sometimes worried if he could accept what they were to learn, she knew he would walk with her through every step, and that gave her comfort; she would not have to face the secrets alone.

"This is your big moment, Sumi," he glowed. "I wouldn't miss it for the world."

The engines' power slackened just before the wheels touched the tarmac, shuddering the cabin inside. The plane quickly slowed down and taxied over to its berth outside the main terminal, coming to a smooth halt. Seatbelts clicked open and overhead bins popped up as vacationers, mostly from Seoul, began eagerly retrieving their belongings and filing towards the exit. Pushing through the crowd seemed to be the custom of choice as Greg attempted to claim the carry-on bags from the luggage bins above. He was tossed back and forth in the hasty stream of passengers squeezing by him.

Soon, Sumi and Greg were inside the terminal and had their luggage loaded onto a cart, which they snaked through the crush of passengers and exited past sliding glass doors. Outside, warm humid air wrapped around them like a blanket. The moisture was so dense they could feel it touching their arms, and sticking their clothes to their skin. A tangerine grove nestled among towering palm trees just outside the airport's main doors welcomed them to their first taste of Korea while all around, hurried passengers were meeting relatives and black taxis were whisking weary travelers off to their hotels.

As they stood watching the bustle, a grinning airport guide with a shiny face approached Greg and, after introducing himself in Korean, asked where they wished to go.

"We're going to the Sunrise Hotel," Greg explained.

"Ahh yeh, Sunrise Hotel, yeh, yeh. Americans?" asked the guide, pointing from Greg to Sumi.

"Yes, that's right," replied Greg.

"Which city?" inquired the guide.

Hesitating, Greg replied: "We're from Los Angeles."

"Ahh, yeh, Los Angeles," the guide smiled, nodding his head vigorously. "First time, Korea?" he continued with wide eyes.

"Yes."

"You like Korea?"

"I'm not sure, we just got here. Now if you can help us, we'd like to go to the Sunrise Hotel. We're very tired."

"I wish you to like Korea," persisted the guide, now holding Greg by the arm. "Very nice country," he gestured in a broad sweep with his free hand. "Jeju Island, very beautiful, yeh. Many volcano rocks, many waterfalls, many fishes."

"Which bus?" injected Sumi.

"Bus? Ahh, yeh, yeh," nodded the guide, smiling and shaking his finger in the air. "Bus number 600. It will go Sunrise Hotel." He pointed at a bus painted red and white, idling some distance away beside the curb.

"Thank you," replied Sumi as Greg quickly filed his cart past the bowing guide.

Once all the luggage was safely tucked beneath, the luxury coach pulled away from the airport and began its cross-island commute. The bus driver had understood nothing but 'Sunrise Hotel' so Sumi and Greg had no idea how long of a journey still lay before them. The tiny cars and vans amused them as they slipped alongside the bus in traffic. Sumi felt scared for the scooter drivers, weaving between lanes and slipping onto sidewalks to pass vehicles, all the while carrying large metal boxes on their backs or between their legs. They reminded her of images she had seen in documentaries describing Asian traffic. A dance with death, she thought.

The city's congestion slowly gave way to countryside speckled with flat-roofed houses and lava-rock walls. These low fences defined farm pasture and enclosed onion crops, palm tree plantations, tangerine groves, and Chinese cabbage gardens. A thousand shades of green covered the land, which was in the midst of full summer production drenched in July's humidity. From one side of the bus, Sumi could see the ocean shimmering far below while on the other, the volcano's peak rose above cotton clouds resting on its shoulders. The highway cut through several of the mountain's roots, exposing steep banks on either side as steel netting held back many of tons of loose rock from swamping the speeding vehicles.

An hour later, the coach hissed to a stop before the palm-treed entrance of the Sunrise Hotel. Walls of stone stretched up to turrets above blushing orange in the sinking sun. Sumi stared in awe from her window at the hotel's ancient yet sumptuous presence; the rounded bricks glistened as though from a recent shower, and stood imposing yet inviting all in the same moment. She followed Greg down the aisle and off the bus where bowing bellhops, arrayed in a crescent before the doors, bowed low and welcomed them to the hotel.

"An-yonha-shimnikka!" they greeted in one voice. Next, their matching green vests and pants hopped into action, unloading luggage, answering questions, and shuttling some guests away in battery-powered golf carts. The entire scene played out with military exactness, leaving Sumi and Greg to stand aside, watch, and wait for them to unload their bags.

Sumi glanced around. The grounds in front of the main entrance were a manicured masterpiece of low hedges and lush lawns surrounding a fountain of creamy marble. From the middle of it leapt three fish spewing thin plumes of water that arched over each other in the air. Two swimming pools, enveloped by thick palm trees, sparkled on the crest of a hill and looked out toward the cliffs and ocean below. Several large lava-stone statues stood guard among the hedges and the trees. They varied in size but were all carved alike: a felt hat, bulging eyes, a flat nose, thin lips forming neither a smile nor a frown, drooping ears, and hands placed gently on the belly. "Harubang," Sumi heard a bellhop say. The 'Grandfather Stones' had been protective deities for Jeju islanders since before recorded history.

Greg and Sumi's luggage soon emerged. An emerald-vested young man pushed it on a cart in front of them and ushered the weary travelers into the main lobby. There, the reservations were confirmed and their cardkeys provided. An eager host directed them to the elevators and, after he proposed a tour of the hotel and they declined due to fatigue, they finally reached their room.

With their luggage sitting exactly where it had been placed, Greg and Sumi both flopped on the bed and immediately plunged into a sound sleep, the kind afforded only to the severely jetlagged.

Sumi slowly opened her eyes. Two small lamps in opposite corners painted the room in a yellow glow while Greg sat in an armchair by the window, watching her with a newspaper in his hand. Outside, night had come and the serenade of insects mixed with the roaring surf.

"Mmm, what a delicious sleep. I could have slept for hours," Sumi purred, stretching her tired arms and shoulders.

"You still can. We have no rush," said Greg.

"I know, and I would too except for my growling stomach. I need to get some food," she replied, shuffling off the bed.

"Do you want room service or should we go out to eat?" he asked, throwing the newspaper onto the table.

"Let's go down to the restaurant," Sumi answered, examining her sleep-deprived and travel-weary hair in the mirror. "I want to experience some culture and besides, room service is so overpriced anyway."

"Sounds good to me. I was actually thinking of getting something myself just before you woke up. What a long trip that was! And how about that obstacle course in Seoul before we could board our plane to get here?"

"I know, that's so strange. I wonder why they would design it like that? Having to completely change airports in order to catch a connecting flight." Sumi slipped her shoes on and followed Greg out of the room.

The hallways were rounded to match the curved face of the castle standing before the ocean. On the left side, doors led to guestrooms that were all touted to offer an unobstructed view of the watery horizon and legendary sunrises. A railing was planted on the other side, and looked out over a nine-story drop to the main floor just beyond the lobby entrance. A white marble sculpture of a Jeju diving woman climbed halfway up the open space while a crystal chandelier reached partway down from the ceiling.

Sumi stood for a moment admiring the view and began to feel dizzy from the height. Below her, the diving woman seemed to be plunging ever deeper into the lobby floor; yet when Sumi looked up, the statue appeared to be reaching for the glimmering crystal above it. Sumi held the railing as they walked to the elevator, and watched the shuttle slide up to their floor. They had been too exhausted to notice earlier that the elevator was made of glass, shaped like a teardrop of light. As it descended to the lobby, the marble statue seemed to grow before Sumi's eyes.

At the bottom, they followed the English and Korean signs to the restaurant, which turned out to be very elegant with dishes available from all over the world and a seafood buffet whose freshness was unmatched. Each table carried a single candle, and the flames' warm glow soaked into the dark interior of the restaurant. They were seated next to the floor-to-ceiling window and the waiter hurried away with their orders.

Outside, the rear lawn extended out to a line of torches burning along the cliff's edge, waving their willowy flames in the night breeze, while in the distance, Sumi and Greg watched white points of light shimmer from the dark ocean. Far out at sea, fishing boats were stabbing their powerful beams into the water to attract fish as they plied their trade through the night.

"Isn't this great, Greg? It's just like being on a second honeymoon," Sumi mused between swallows of her sole fillet.

"This feels better than our first one. We're not strapped for cash, and we don't have to visit the in-laws," Greg grinned.

"I wonder what Mama's honeymoon was like here? Everything must have looked so much different 50 years ago. We should see if they have any historical information available about the hotel in the 1950's. Maybe they even have a guest list or something. That would help us learn what this place was like back then."

"I would think they'd have some artifacts. At least some pictures showing the progress of the hotel. Everything around here has obviously been renovated recently, probably for the 2002 World Cup. What an incredible time that was for Korea! Remember those street cheerers on TV, Sumi? I just about went crazy watching those games."

"You did, Greg. I was there."

Just then, a man in a dark suit and a gold tie approached their table. "Good evening, I'm very sorry to interrupt. My name is Tony Choi," he announced, bowing courteously. "I am a part owner of the hotel." His black hair was combed back in parallel strokes, and he spoke in well-articulated English. "I am aware that you are from America?"

"Yes, that's right. Word seems to travel fast around here," Greg replied.

"I always take a keen interest in the welfare of my guests. I do trust you have been well treated?" he asked, looking from Greg to Sumi with concern rippling on his dark eyebrows.

"Everything's fine, thank you," smiled Sumi.

"Very nice," Greg offered.

"Excellent. I would hate for you to come all this way and something be amiss. Is there anything you need, anything special I can arrange for you?"

"Actually, we were just talking about that," Sumi began, gesturing to Greg. "We were wondering if you might have some historical documents or pictures from the earlier days of the hotel."

"That's very possible. I might be able to dig something up for you from the vault. May I ask: is your ancestry Korean?" Tony pointed from Sumi to Greg.

"Actually, I was born in Korea but I immigrated to America as a child with my parents. I have very few memories from here," answered Greg.

"Well, what a perfect opportunity to return and create some! And I assume you are of Korean descent as well?" Tony asked, turning to Sumi.

"I was born in the States but yes, both my parents were Korean too. They actually came here, to this very hotel, for their honeymoon many years ago. That's why we have come to visit," Sumi returned, smiling.

"What a fascinating story!" exclaimed Tony. He clasped his hands together excitedly and held them in front of him. "I suppose that makes this just about a family reunion then. Well, I must be going. Again, I am very sorry for intruding. I will leave you to your dinner while I do some research into those historical documents you'd like to see. Please, enjoy your evening," he entreated, folding slightly at the waist.

"Thank you, we will," replied Sumi, watching him turn and walk away. "What a kind gesture that was," she wondered, returning to her fillet. "To think how big this hotel is and he still makes time to pay such personal attention to his guests."

"It all seems pretty oily to me," Greg replied. "Makes me wonder what he was really after."

"Oh, Greg! Would you stop it and just relax for a minute? He was only being friendly, like a good host should. You've got to stop suspecting people always have a hidden agenda behind everything they do."

"I'm just saying it seems a bit odd, like he was fishing for information. This hotel is huge, and I'm positive we're not the only foreigners here. But you like him so maybe he is all right. I just thought he was laying it on a bit thick, that's all."

"Well, maybe that's the way things are done here. It doesn't really matter. And besides, he might be our best help in finding some information about the Sunrise Hotel Mama saw and stayed in."

Greg watched Sumi's eyes sparkle in the candlelight as she glanced around the restaurant. The flame seemed to burn motionless from within her chest and flush her cheeks with red fire. When her eyes returned to his, he spoke to them: "Sumi, I have a bit of a surprise to tell you."

"Really? What?" She leaned forward with her elbows on the table and looked over the candle at Greg.

"Well, it's about your mom and us coming here. Do you remember her last day? When we were both at the hospital together?" Greg pushed his plate aside and leaned ahead as well.

"Yes, of course."

"And do you remember when she called me back in the room when we had almost left?"

"Yeah, and I went down to the car by myself."

"Well, your mom didn't really need me to fix her pillows. When I got back to her bed, I started helping her and she suddenly grabbed my arm tightly. Her grip was unbelievable, like steel. She pulled me down so that I was staring her straight in the eye, and she said: 'Greg, I haven't long in this world. I probably won't even be here tomorrow. I want you to take this envelope.'

Then she paused for breath, reached into a drawer next to her bed and pulled out a brown package. It was all wrapped up with string and tape. She handed it to me, and I remember her saying: 'I couldn't tell Sumi everything today, though I had meant to. I have kept all of it hidden inside for so long that I had no way of bringing it out. But this package holds some very important pieces of our past. I don't want you to tell Sumi anything about it until you both open it in your room at the Sunrise Hotel, promise?' She made me promise to her right there. And I've kept the package with me this entire year. It's actually packed away in my carry-on upstairs."

"You never said a word," breathed Sumi, sitting back in her chair with her arms folded in front of her.

"Your mom made me promise, Sumi, and then she was gone that night. She knew what my word meant to me, that's why she made me promise, and it's always been something I felt I should honour. I'm sorry if this upsets you, sweetheart. But the package is still unopened, exactly the way your mom sealed it, and it has waited until precisely the time she had set for it."

Greg slid his card into the door and pushed the handle down, letting Sumi in first. From the bottom of his backpack he pulled a bulging envelope sealed with several layers of clear tape over string. He handed the package to Sumi who began slowly cutting away the bonds. When she had finished slicing open the paper, she laid it flat on the bed and a mound of black and white photographs spilled out, as well as some faded letters and notes. Sumi started picking through them.

"Oh my, Greg! Look at this. That's Mama as a girl. I recognize her from the picture she always kept by her bed, the one with her mom and dad and the farm. But I wonder who this boy is standing beside her?" She pointed at the worn photo.

"Maybe she had a brother," Greg mused, looking over her shoulder.

"Oh here, it has some writing on the back," she exclaimed, flipping the picture over. "Byun Shin-char. I wonder who that was?"

Sumi picked up another photograph and read the back first. "Here it says that these are Mama's parents, my grandparents. I've never heard anything about them," she said, inspecting their faces closely.

Greg selected a worn picture from the pile and Sumi examined the writing. "And here's one of Mama's mother and grandmother," she announced, flipping the picture over to see a shrunken woman with a bent back and bowed legs hunching beside a younger woman.

Sumi kept sorting through the photographs and realized that most of the people and names she could not recognize. They were all strangers to her, unrelated from another time. She felt no connection to the landscape or the faces portrayed in the faded relics.

Near the bottom of the pile, she found a special picture. "Greg, look! It's Mama's wedding photo!"

The portrait was in perfect condition as though it had never seen light or air. Before a background of painted midnight, a young woman in a brilliant white hanbok stood with one arm resting on the back of a chair. Her dark hair spooled on top of her head and a jeweled necklace rested on her shoulders, as diamonds on satin. She wasn't smiling; rather, on first glance, her face was somber and her eyes a melancholy well. And yet the corners of her mouth and the edges of her lips brought mirth to light, and fought with the overall serious tone of the picture. A man wearing a black suit sat beside her in the chair, his hands spread over his knees and his mouth a thin line. His eyes burned like black fire from the center of the portrait; dark eyebrows curved down towards a stiff nose, and his hair held its shape without a strand out of place. His posture was rigid, his hands hard, and his face handsome and cold. For 50 years, he had sat in complete obscurity until now, finally being exposed to his only daughter.

"You want me to sit? Shouldn't she sit and I stand? That way I'm the taller as the man of the house," said the groom in the dark suit.

"This is the way all the wedding portraits are being done these days. It is a seat of honour, as kings and rulers always sit. But you can have it however you like," informed the photographer as he arranged the lighting.

"No, that sounds good. I will sit."

The photographer eyed the wedded pair through his lens and circled around the small studio again, readjusting the filters and backdrop, and shifting several lights so they better illuminated his subjects. "You make a very beautiful couple," he said as he bustled about.

"Thank you," the groom answered as the bride looked up from the brown beetle she had watched lumber across the studio floor. "Why don't you put your hand on my shoulder?" he whispered, glancing back at her with scowl. "Are you so afraid to touch me?"

He reached back and pulled her hand from the back of the chair onto his shoulder.

"Now, you can keep a serious expression, or you can smile. Both are being done," the photographer informed, returning to his tripod.

"We won't smile. And could you hurry up? We don't have much time," spat the groom. Then turning to whisper to his bride, he breathed: "I thought I told you to put your hand on my shoulder?"

She replaced her hand only after several more whispered threats.

"Of course, you're going to have to look at me and not talk if you want this done quickly," the photographer chided from behind his camera.

"Take it," growled the groom as he stared at the photographer with eyes like a smoldering fire. His bride beside him smirked and, unknown to the groom, lifted her hand and placed it on the chair as the lights exploded before them.

Sumi examined the photograph closely, staring at her father's chiseled face. With her left hand, she rubbed her moist eyes and continued to stare at the picture. "That's my dad," she whispered finally. "How I've wondered what he was like and now here he is. I wish I could have known him." She ran her finger down the picture. "Seeing him here, now, makes me feel like I've missed so much of who I am."

They continued to sort through the pile of personal documents containing some letters between Mama and her friends, old newspaper clippings, and pictures of Los Angeles during the 1950's and 60's. Sumi was astounded by the wealth of information confronting her, like she was discovering a past of someone she never knew.

Greg sorted through the stack and found a smaller envelope, crisp and white but bulging with its contents. *Hangul*, Korean writing, was scribbled over the front of it.

"Take a look at this, Sumi," he said as he handed it over.

Sumi read the inscription. "This is Mama's writing. She says this is what she's been keeping from me all these years." She paused. "But I can only open it after we take a complete tour of the hotel and grounds. I wonder what it could be? Here at the bottom it says to pay close attention to the cliffs by the ocean."

"Looks like we're going to have to take that tour after all," Greg yawned, lying back on the bed and stretching. "In the meantime, we should try to get some sleep and adjust to the time change."

They both gathered up the strewn pictures and papers and placed them in a heap beside the TV. Crawling under the light linen covers, Sumi and Greg were dreaming before their eyes fell shut.

three

The morning was quickly passing by the time Sumi and Greg awoke. The sky was cloudless and a warm ocean breeze played with the curtains on their balcony. Birds and insects were chattering furiously outside their window but behind everything, as a sonic background, they could hear the ever-present growling of the surf.

"It's a beautiful day," Greg mumbled, climbing out of bed. He slowly reached his arms towards the ceiling. "I still feel tired but I guess we should get out there and enjoy this." He ambled over to the balcony, and stepped through the flitting curtains.

"It's gorgeous indeed. I'm going to have a shower and get ready," Sumi replied, stretching and rubbing the sleep from her eyes.

She passed by the table and spotted her mother's wedding photo. It was partly covered by some other pictures so that only her father was visible. As she glanced at him, she realized she carried many of his facial features; she had his face shape, eyes, and nose at least. She had never thought she looked much like her mother, and now she knew why. I must have reminded Mama of him all these years, she thought. She held the photo beside her face as she looked into the mirror, and saw the similarity was striking, especially in the eyes.

Still watching the reflection, Sumi's gaze passed to her mother's young form standing beside the chair, and suddenly her mind was jarred with the shadow of a dream that yet lingered in the closets of her mind. She closed her eyes and desperately tried to remember what she had seen in her sleep. Several moments later, an image, still unclear with the webs of slumber, crept into her consciousness from some dark recess of her brain: a young woman in a white hanbok walked slowly amid a swirling storm, the wind tearing at her dress as it swept past. Her soaked hair was piled high on her head with wet strands tumbling down and tossing around in the rain.

Keeping her eyes welded shut, Sumi sat back heavily on the bed behind her and held her head in her hands as the recollection of the dream intensified. She hadn't recognized the woman while the dream-birthed images had played in her sleep, but now she knew her without mistake. The storm lashed the bride's frail body as she walked along the cliff's edge, and the darkness, enveloping beside and behind, threatened to swallow her into its abysmal belly.

Suddenly, as though the night sky had been lifted like a lid, thin rays of light pierced through the gloom and lit the entire ocean and shoreline with white gold. The wind and gnashing darkness pealed back before the onslaught, and the woman was left alone on the edge of the world facing a vast, azure sea. As the sun rose and the land around her grew brighter, the lonely bride seemed to absorb the light until it began passing into her dress and body, and then through them like water through a sieve. The last vision Sumi had seen before waking was the woman glowing with solar fire and joining the rays of the sun as it passed overhead, far above the rocky shores and tattered shreds of cloud on the horizon.

"That's a fantastic picture," said Greg, stepping inside from the balcony and seeing Sumi on the bed holding the wedding photo. "They really were quite a stunning couple."

"I had a dream," Sumi whispered, still staring down at the picture.

"Oh, me too!" he called. "Must be the traveling. I dreamed we were flying for hours on this tiny plane and they wouldn't serve us any food. They kept saying we'd have to wait longer and I was starving! What was yours about?"

"I'm not sure," Sumi replied softly, looking at her mother's smooth face and silky dress.

"Oh, I just hate that, when you forget what your dream was. And it always seems like no matter how hard you try, you can never quite recapture it when you're awake. What do you say we go get some breakfast?"

Sumi stood and looked over at Greg standing by the window, bare-chested and in his underwear. Without a word, she put the picture down on the dresser and continued to the bathroom.

"What?" Greg called as she pulled the door shut.

After breakfast, they passed by the front desk where the clerk relayed the message that Mr. Choi wished to meet with them in his office. They were directed to the third floor, west end of the hallway. There, a heavy oak door opened on a spacious office wrapped with windows. Statues and carvings from all over the world stood scattered about the room.

"Please come in," Tony invited, rising from behind his spacious desk. "I'm delighted to see you were able to make it. Please, have a seat," he offered, and motioned towards the leather couch opposite his desk on the ocean side of the office. The window looked out upon the entire rear expanse of the hotel grounds, and towards a small island with sheer walls a short distance from shore.

"I've been looking through our archives and I have found two files so far that might be of interest to you," began Tony. He lifted a large brown box onto the desk from behind his chair. "One has photographs dating from before the renovation of 1973, and the other contains the many guest books from 1953 onwards." He piled a second box beside the first one. "Now, when did you say your parents had their honeymoon here?"

"I'm actually not sure," replied Sumi sheepishly. "I know that probably sounds strange, but I've never learned the exact date. I believe they were married sometime in the early 50's."

"During the Korean War?" asked Tony.

"Yes, that's right. My father was killed in that war, and my mom fled to America shortly after."

Tony paused and rubbed his forehead with two fingers, pinching the skin between his eyebrows. "The opening of this hotel was actually postponed by that war. It was originally built in the years following the Second World War, but the onset of battle with communists on the peninsula pushed the opening back two years."

He dug through the first box and retrieved two thick albums with rounded spines. "Here are some pictures of the various construction phases," he explained, circling around his desk and delivering a leather-bound photo album to Sumi. "And this one contains shots of the hotel in its earliest form," he added, pushing the other edition to the edge of his desk.

Greg and Sumi began flipping through the pictorial evolution of the region. The first book held mostly poor quality photographs, but did manage to convey the state of the area at the birth of the hotel. The second album contained much better pictures, and portrayed a majestic resort equipped with very advanced features for its time. The main building was only a fraction of the size of the present hotel, but included an additional, smaller structure standing by itself near the ocean.

"What's this house out front here?" asked Greg, pointing at a picture in a promotional brochure from the 1960's.

"That was the honeymoon suite, which only the original hotel had. It was demolished in the renovations of 1973 that expanded the central structure and created a park and fountain where the guesthouse had stood. It was a bold touch in the 50's to have a luxury suite separate from the main building. It was famous in its day but didn't last. Depending on how much money they were willing to spend, perhaps your parents stayed in that very suite," Tony gestured at Sumi.

"I'm not sure, but I guess it's possible they did," she answered, her thoughts sweeping through the photos she had seen of her parents.

"Maybe we'll be able to find out later," Tony offered. "Now, here is the very first guest book, August – November 1953." He pulled a heavy, tan manual from the second box, and opened it onto the desk. The pages parted stiffly with their faded gold trim glinting in the sun.

The young lady trembled as she picked up the quill and scrawled her name on the line. The ink ran freely from the tip, and she signed quickly to avoid blotches from forming on the pristine paper. Once finished, she handed the pen to her husband who pushed past her and scratched his name and hometown on the line below hers. She looked over his curved back at the clerk behind the counter. He smiled softly at her, but her eyes stared back at him in fear, wincing at her husband's every movement. As he admired his signature, her husband noticed that his name now scrawled below hers on the page. With a flurry, he blurred her name from the scroll. "Sign again," he said, throwing the feathered pen at the book.

"However, before we look at these," Tony interrupted, placing his hand on the cover of the album of signatures, "I was wondering if you would prefer to take a tour of the grounds so you can get an idea of the area. Unless, of course, you've already had a look around. I'll be able to show you this material after."

"No, we haven't had a chance yet," answered Sumi. "That sounds fine."

"Let's take this second album along and we'll try to pinpoint some landscape features," he suggested, rising from his chair.

Leading Sumi and Greg out of the hotel, Tony brought them along winding paths past the fountain, the pools and the statues, and out towards the ocean. The pine trees spread along the cliff's edge stood proud and straight as they dug their roots deep into the ground to prevent them from falling over the sheer wall. A cement barrier also ran the entire way among the trees to protect guests from accidentally plunging down to the surf and rocks below.

Tony described the modern spread of the hotel, and the boundaries where it had stood in its infancy. He talked about the honeymoon suite, how it had been the favourite of South Korea's first president, and how it had attracted the wealthy and famous when they came to visit Jeju.

Later, they enjoyed the view from cliffs where they could admire block-shaped Tiger Island out at sea while to the north, rising behind the hotel and wrapped in cloud, stood the volcanic peak of

Mt. Halla, South Korea's highest mountain. Directly to the west sat the harbour, and beyond it billowed the white sail roof of the Seogwipo World Cup stadium. Tony directed them to look below, across a tiny cove, where a small waterfall plunged several meters into the sea. "It's only a trickle now but during times of heavy rain, it falls in a beautiful silver sheet that pounds at the ocean's edge," he explained. "Many guests like to bathe in it during the summer months, and it's even believed to have healing properties for arthritis and backaches."

Looking through the evergreens and across the small bay, Greg noticed a cave burrowed into the cliff face beside the waterfall. "What's that hole in the rock down there?" he asked.

"That is a very unique feature of Jeju. It's the entrance to one of the many lava tubes that snake beneath the island. They were formed thousands of years ago when the volcano was still active. Lava on the island's surface cooled and hardened first while still running molten underneath, creating underground rivers of magma. These eventually cooled too, leaving an empty 'lava tube', this one with its doorway facing the Pacific Ocean. The tide rises almost to its threshold but is never invited in, except a small trickle during more violent storms."

He paused, put his finger on his lips, and then beckoned them closer. "Have you ever heard about the snake gods of Jeju?" he asked in a hushed voice.

Greg and Sumi both shook their heads as they leaned in with widened eyes.

"It's a legend that's been told to every Jeju child for countless generations," he continued in a whisper as his dark eyebrows shifted nervously between Sumi and Greg. "Thousands of years ago, the snake gods issued from that and other caves on the island to seize any unlucky villagers that happened to be nearby. They would then drag them back to their lairs to consume them at their leisure. These serpent spirits were as enormous as they were ferocious; the people stood no chance at defending themselves. They found the only way to appease the viper gods was to make a sacrifice to them, a young virgin maiden between 14 and 16 years old. When the snake lords received the poor girl's life, all attacks on the islanders would halt for one year, at which time they would require another sacrifice. They dwelt under the island in the many lava tubes cutting through it, and they received their power from the mother adder who would coil up her girth in the belly of the volcano itself."

Tony pointed again to the summit of Mt. Halla, now a blue crown fenced by rose cloud.

"That's why every cave entrance on the island is either far from habitation or, as in the case of this one, has only recently been developed." His voice was barely audible now. "And it's been said if you venture too far into the caves, you can sometimes hear the ghosts of the poor sacrificed girls wailing from somewhere under the island. Needless to say, only two caves on Jeju are open to the public and these are used exclusively by tourists. Mystique flows deep here and is not easily forgotten."

Sumi shuddered and Greg glanced back at the dark oval eye staring out from the rock below. As the sparkling blue water threw white foam up to it, Sumi wondered what secrets that strange tunnel held captive in its black throat.

The three of them continued along the cliff edge until they came to a stone plaque standing at the foremost lookout point.

"What does this say, Sumi?" Greg asked, squinting at the writing.

"It's something about a bride who died on this spot in 1953." Sumi's voice slowed. "And her ghost has been seen in this area ever since."

She turned to Tony. "What's this about, Mr. Choi?"

Warm rain fell. A fierce wind from the ocean whipped over the cliffs and sent the rain lashing against the rocks and trees while lightning again ignited the night sky, illuminating two figures facing each other near the cliff's edge. The woman stood with her back against the wooden railing that looked out over the angry sea far below while in front of her, the man advanced slowly, now no more than five steps away. The woman continued screaming at him and still the wind swept her words away, drowning them in the rain. The man took another step forward. Backing farther away from him, the woman climbed over the railing and held the soaked wood between her fingers as the wind tried to shred her clothes from her body and the furious waves pounded the rocks below.

The woman screamed again. This time several words fled above the gale: "I … never be … bride!" Suddenly, the man lunged forward but grasped only empty wind. The woman had already let go of the railing and fallen backwards from the cliff. The man gripped the wood and saw her plummet for a moment before the raging surf covered over her and she was no more.

The sun was growing hot as Tony dabbed his forehead with a handkerchief. "This is an interesting story, and has even become our very own legend here at the Sunrise Hotel. A honeymooning couple stayed with us during the hotel's first month of operation, August 1953. They were the first actual honeymooners to stay in the guesthouse. During their wedding night, a violent typhoon descended upon the island, the kind that often sweep through here at that time of year. The way the story goes, the bride had wanted to go for a walk in the storm wearing her wedding hanbok; so they both put on their marriage attire and went out in the raging wind and rain. Somehow, in the darkness, she came too close to the edge. At that time, there was no railing that covered the entire perimeter, only certain open places. She fell from this very spot to her death on the rocks below."

Tony gestured at the vertical drop to sea level just a few steps away.

"The hotel staff was unable to attempt a rescue that night because the only way to the bottom of the cliff, other than jumping, is down the stairs back there by the lava tube cave and waterfall. With the storm and high tide hitting at the same time, the way was blocked. In the morning, the only trace of her that was found was the hanbok, all bloodied and torn. They suspected sharks or some other sea creatures had taken the body after ripping the dress open. Or perhaps it was swept out to sea. Nobody really knows for sure.

However, the story doesn't end there. In the months and years following the tragedy, many people claimed to see the bride's ghost, or feel its presence. It always wears a white hanbok with wet hair pinned up high on its head, and it's said to float with the wind along the edge of the cliff during stormy nights to keep people from wandering too close and falling over. But it has been seen other places too, like the corridors in the west end of the hotel, in the middle of the lawn over there, and sometimes down by the waterfall and cave. Some people have even said it helped them, or kept them from danger in certain situations.

And to date, everyone who has ever claimed any contact with it has always said he or she felt better after seeing the ghost or knowing it was there. Sometimes people have come to the hotel contemplating suicide and have left with renewed hope and sense of purpose. There's a long list of devotees who say their lives have improved because of their stay at the Sunrise and their experience with the ghost. It has even brought curiosity seekers and paranormal types from around the world to see if they can learn anything from it. But these have all gone away disappointed and empty-handed. The spirit seems to know who genuinely needs help and who is just searching for sensationalism because it has never revealed itself to a camera, a video, a tape recorder, or anyone trying to expose it. It simply seems to know who to trust. Whatever it is, it has sure been a real blessing for us, not a curse."

As Tony spoke, Sumi felt her ribs tighten around her heart and her breath sat trapped in her throat. Twice her dream passed through her mind in vivid colour before he had finished.

"That's incredible!" Greg exclaimed. "When was the last time it was seen?"

"It's actually been quite a while. I can't remember exactly but I'm sure no one has mentioned seeing or feeling it for about a year now."

Sumi forced her mouth open and her words fell haltingly from her lips. "What was the bride's name?" she asked.

"Park Un-hee."

Sumi gasped and staggered slightly while staring at Tony in disbelief. Greg grabbed her arm to steady her. "What's wrong, Sumi?"

"Are you all right?" asked Tony.

"Mr. Choi, that's my mother's name."

Tony, Sumi and Greg hurried back to the hotel and into Tony's office. He snatched the guest book from his desk and flipped to the very beginning, the first month of the hotel's existence. After several pages of dignitaries' and military officials' signatures, the ordinary guest roll began. Tony ran his finger down the page and stopped just below an entry that had been scratched over with ink.

"This was her husband, Kim Ju-han from Gwanju City. And just below is her name, Park Un-hee. Her hometown was Jeju City, on the north side of the island. She signed this book upon entering the hotel, and she fell from the cliffs that very night. Now you say your mother has the same name?"

"Yes. I believe she was born near Jeju City, and she said that she stayed at this hotel on her honeymoon, which, I assume, was sometime in the early 50's."

"And you never knew the exact date?"

"No, my mom never spoke of her past. This is as much as I know."

"Do you know if this is your father's name?"

"No, I never knew him. I only know he died in the Korean War shortly after they were married."

"After they were married? Hmm, let me think," Tony mused, stroking his cheek and staring at the guest book. After a moment, he looked up again. "It all sounds very odd because the Korean War was over by the time this hotel opened. The

41

inauguration, which was planned for June of 1952, was postponed until August 12, 1953 when it became essentially a victory celebration to toast the end of the war. The signing of the armistice agreement in July made it all possible. If this Park Un-hee was indeed your mother, then she and her husband were the very first honeymooning couple to stay in the guesthouse that night of August 12, and that was definitely after the war. But the Park Un-hee who signed this book was also the one who fell from the cliff and died in the stormy ocean that same night. I'm sorry if this has caused any confusion."

Sumi looked from the book to Tony, and finally to Greg, doubt growing in her eyes. Her trembling lips parted slightly. "I'm sorry," she breathed as she turned towards the door and slipped out down the hall.

Greg followed behind her.

Inside the hotel room, Sumi wept bitterly face down on the bed. Her body shook as she drew air down to fill the salty vacuum in her chest. "We never should have come. Now I have more questions about everything than I ever had," she sobbed. "And more doubt about what the truth really is. I know Mama was really my mom. That is a fact that will not change no matter what anybody tells me or shows me." She reached for a tissue from the end table. "But who is this poor soul with the same name who died on her wedding night, if it's not her? I'm so confused."

"It's ok, honey," Greg stroked her hair and pulled her close to him. "I don't know either but I know we're going to find out."

He looked out toward the blue water dancing with the diamonds of the afternoon sun. "Sometimes answers come in pieces, and right now the pieces don't all seem to fit together. But hold onto what you know to be true, Sumi."

"What is true, Greg?" she replied, looking up at him with stung eyes. "That's my whole problem, I don't know what the truth is anymore."

"Well, we still have this envelope from your mom to go through. Maybe it will tell us more about what really happened here."

"I forgot about that one," Sumi said, wiping her cheeks. She walked over to the dresser and picked it up. Looking at it as it lay in her hands and seeing her mother's writing on the front, she suddenly felt as though she carried the weight of many worlds in that tiny package. "You open it," she blurted, handing it Greg. "I don't want to see it first."

Carefully ripping open the sealed letter, he retrieved several handwritten pages wrapped around a single photograph. He pulled it from between the scripted sheets and both he and Sumi examined it.

"As the first newlywed couple at the hotel, we would be honoured if you would pose for a picture in our main lobby."

"Splendid! Un-hee, come this way," Ju-han instructed, pulling her beside him. She followed silently with her head bowed, holding the bow of her white hanbok between her fingers as it gleamed under the chandeliers.

They entered the spacious lobby and stood together in front of the fountain in the middle. Ju-han held tightly to her arm and pulled her close to him. Just then, lightning flashed outside, followed by a crack of thunder. Un-hee shuddered at the sudden noise.

"Looks like a storm is moving in for the night," mused the photographer, adjusting the camera on the tripod.

"I want you to smile and look your best now, right?" whispered Ju-han as he adjusted his suit jacket with his free hand.

"That's looks perfect. You make such a beautiful couple. Ready now, one, two, three… smile!"

The flash bulb burst with light as the camera snapped the picture.

"Excellent," praised the photographer.

"They both look so happy," Greg said. "It's a beautiful photo. Seems like it was taken right here in the hotel."

Sumi stared at the bride. She was radiant. Even after 50 years, her smile was dazzling, and her hanbok, sculpted as though it were made of snow, elevated the entire atmosphere of the photo from a simple marble foyer to heavenly fountain. The longer Sumi looked, the less she saw. Soon, her gaze centered on the bride's eyes. A dark well lay within her pupils, a deep and guarded storehouse of secrets that drowned all who risked venturing too close. This stronghold was easily hid by her playful mouth and smooth skin, both of which held too much promise on the surface to betray any shadowy depths beneath. Sumi handed the picture back to Greg and closed her eyes.

Replacing the photo in the envelope, he unfolded the handwritten sheets. There were many, and they had obviously been penned with great care since the writing was tiny and clung to both sides of each page. The script was entirely *hangul*, so he handed them to Sumi who started translating.

Their story, which revealed Sumi's past, was written by Park Un-hee, Sumi's mother, the only person who ever knew the entire tale, and she had held it as a prisoner in her heart until several days before her death when she had penned these pages.

Timo Annala

Part II

four

The carriage was as black as a moonless winter midnight, carrying silver trim and wooden wheels. The stallions pulling it were birthed from the self-same night, except for patches of white on their foreheads and the chrome blinders they wore on their eyes. Under a hot dry sky, they toiled over uneven roads weaving through the forests on the volcano's east side. The driver barked at them from his perch above while inside the wagon, a newlywed couple, suffering through the heat and bumpy ride, sat alone together for the first time.

Once in a while, the bride's head would hit the window next to her when the carriage struck a larger bump in the road. She leaned her shoulder against the wall while her other arm stretched away from her towards the other side of the wagon. At the end of it, her fingers felt as still as ice inside her husband's sweaty grip. He pushed her hand away and she laid it cold on her lap, though August's heat smothered her skin. Her body felt sticky inside her hanbok, and she wished more breeze would blow in through the side windows. Lifting her eyes, she glanced out at the indigo sky outside. Above her, heaven's roof was clear and distant; yet when she gazed ahead, dark clouds crept higher over the trees as an advancing blanket of shadow from the sea.

Suddenly, the carriage lurched violently around a corner, and the horses' hooves clattered along the stones as the driver's whip cracked down on them from above.

"Hey! When will we get there?" shouted Ju-han through the small opening behind the driver. "We've been bouncing back here long enough!"

"Shortly, sir," returned the driver, again yelling and whipping at the horses.

Ju-han sat back down next to Un-hee and took her hand in his moist clutch again. "Soon we'll be at the hotel, my bride. I'm sure it's the nicest one you've ever seen. We'll be able to enjoy ourselves properly there, right?" His words sank to Un-hee like lead from his mouth.

"Yes, Ju-han. Of course," Un-hee melted in reply.

Ju-han's lips pulled back into a satisfied grin, revealing a space between his front two teeth. Un-hee stared through their black gap before turning back to the window that now showed the ocean spread like an immense blue carpet below. The face of the water was pale but darkened with every passing moment. Soon, it disappeared behind a curtain of trees as the forest swallowed the carriage, bouncing down towards the coast.

Un-hee watched the trees blur by in a wall of green, dark closets hiding between the staccato of cedar and pine. She saw the lowest day of her life flash past in vivid colour, preceded by her father's cold eyes that had told her he was forcing her to marry Ju-han, though she did not love him. She had begged him to relent but would have had greater success pleading with a stone; he would not listen. Finally, she had watched his upper lip curl back when she had tried to reveal to him the true nature of Ju-han's family.

"I don't mean to disobey you, papa," she had said. "I will marry anyone else, anyone you can find. But not him. Please, papa, not Kim Ju-han. His family destroyed ours; his father is evil. He is responsible for mama being taken by the Japanese army during the war. He is responsible for her pain and death, don't you see? How can you be so blind?"

Un-hee knew Ju-han's father had been a traitor to the Korean people in the vilest fashion. Years ago, he had collaborated with the Japanese army and had arranged for countless women, including Un-hee's mother, to disappear beneath the shadow of Japanese occupation. These daughters and sisters and mothers had been subjected to a most heinous brutality, serving as sex slaves for the Japanese forces, and Un-hee's mother had lived, suffered, and died among them. Un-hee had learned all this following her father's choice to wed her with Ju-han, but because she could not reveal the identity of her informant, her father took it as a lie of disobedience.

"You have a lying, filthy mouth!" he had raged. "You will marry him!"

The walls had seemed closer and smaller around Un-hee as he advanced towards her. "You will marry him or I have no daughter! His family is prominent and wealthy. This marriage will bring honour to you and your family. Are you so selfish that you would rather shame me, though I have done everything, even laid down my own life for you, than marry this man and fulfill your duty? You ungrateful daughter!"

He had shaken his fist before Un-hee's face.

"You were ready to defy me to marry that Shin-char, but thankfully the war took him. Now you're still trying to disobey me by creating lies about this upstanding family. You wretch, you will marry Ju-han!"

His eyes of fire had burned above her as she hid in that corner, and one more word from her mouth would have brought down punishing fists. She accepted her sentence like death and the day of wedded vows had followed two months later.

But Un-hee still clung to Shin-char's memory. Her heart had been his ever since they played together as children outside her house on rain-soaked afternoons. The happiest moments she could remember circled around her mother, her grandmother, and him: chasing each other through cabbage fields, playing games in tangerine groves, learning the proper funeral rites for respecting their ancestors, the 'Honoured Dead', during the various holidays throughout the year. Sometimes on hot summer days, they would swim in the cool creek near Un-hee's home, or run down the lane to the ocean and push each other off the rocks that formed the jagged coastline. In winter, they would brave the chilling wind to watch the diving women collecting clams and mollusks, and then race back to Un-hee's house to savour the stew and rice her mother had prepared. Even now, whenever she thought of her childhood, memories of Shin-char, her mother and grandmother filled her heart with such pleasing scents that she couldn't imagine a more blissful existence.

Then terror struck. Several months after Un-hee's seventh birthday, her mother was torn from her weeping eyes as Japanese army officers forced her into a black truck wrapped in a black tarp. She remembered hearing her father's piercing scream, and seeing him rush forward until the butt of a Japanese rifle smashed him in the face. He continued to struggle until more rifles had beaten him into submission on the dusty ground. Her grandmother had cowered inside the doorway, and Un-hee had hid behind her until she heard the truck snarl and speed away down the lane. Though that was the last time she had ever seen her mother, Un-hee's heart ached for her as though she had left yesterday.

However, her grief was only just crossing the threshold of sorrows. Before the following winter ended, her grandmother grew weaker and thinner until death stole her one frigid morning. The wrinkled face had smiled at Un-hee until the end, and though she never learned what sickness had taken her, she forever suspected a heart too full of anguish to function.

Some dark years later, Shin-char was also ripped from her life and called to battle the communists of North Korea in the war. Before he left, he had pledged himself to her as a soul divided until it could be joined with hers forever. His passionate correspondence continued while bombs fell and battles raged, and Un-hee readied herself for his joyful return. He wanted to marry her as soon as he was released since they both felt growing opposition from Un-hee's father, and knew the longer they tarried, the more opportunity he had to betroth her to someone else.

Shin-char's duty had officially ended six months ago, but only a stained letter ever arrived at Un-hee's door. The army had extended his service time, and had called him to another offensive in the mountains northeast of Seoul. Shin-char had no idea when he would be discharged, but his letter remained optimistic and he promised that he would be hers for all time. He desired to be married the very day he finally returned to Jeju, and he even penned a poem for her, the only one he ever wrote. Less than 3 weeks later, his snowbound company was ambushed by North Korean forces and Shin-char, who had been placed at the front line of battle by his commanding officer, fell for the last time along with four fellow soldiers.

Un-hee felt her hand fold inside a tightening grip.

"I am no fool, my bride," Ju-han's hot breath broke into her thoughts. "I know that you were less than thrilled about our union. But now we are one. You are my bride, today and always. And as such, I expect you to show the proper respect and poise since you are now part of my family. I can overlook your little show today at the studio if you learn your place in this world, to treat others around you according to the level you now possess. And I know you will soon learn my position as the man and head of the house. I'm sure you understand."

Ju-han looked down at Un-hee in the growing gloom of the wagon.

She did not look up; instead, she stared straight ahead at the black carriage wall. Curling her fingers into a fist, she wrenched her hand from Ju-han's grip.

"I am Park Un-hee and I am no different now than I have always been. Marrying you changes nothing in me. I will continue to treat people according to what they deserve, not what their status might be."

Ju-han reached over and bound both her arms together in iron fingers. She winced under his power. "You will do as I say." His words hissed through clenched teeth. "That is the first and most important lesson you will learn." He stood up and hunched over her under the low ceiling, tightening his hold even more. "You will obey me, woman."

The carriage jolted and started rumbling faster down the hill. Ju-han and Un-hee were tossed from one end to the other inside the wagon, and Ju-han had to release Un-hee's arms to steady himself against the wall.

"What's going on out there?" yelled Ju-han.

"Hold on, folks! I lost the reins but I'll have them back in a second," the driver called.

Amid Ju-han's curses, Un-hee braced herself against the bench and watched from the window as the horses surged ever faster down the lane, their hooves pounding the earth. The forest fell away from the edge of the road and a high wall of black stone bricks flashed past. Behind it, a field of grass opened around the carriage and stretched wide on either side. The stallions continued plunging along the road towards the hotel, standing like a castle at the far end of the green expanse. The walls of stone grew from the grass and were crowned with turrets that looked to the four winds of heaven. The lead sky above had mixed with inky clouds and now matched the dark rock of the castle.

Suddenly, the charging horses dug their hooves into the gravel and the carriage lurched to a stop. Un-hee and Ju-han slammed against the opposite wall inside as dust billowed around the wagon and covered the windows with brown soot. The horses were snorting and stamping outside, and Un-hee could hear men shouting from some distance away. Ju-han pushed open the door, reached above, and pulled the stricken driver down from his perch. As Un-hee stumbled down the carriage steps, several of the hotel's staff were rushing to separate the two men.

"You're not fit to drive an ox cart, you drunken fool!" screamed Ju-han while three employees tried to hold him back.

"Sir! Please calm down, sir!" the bellhops shouted.

"Enough!" a deep voice called above the din.

Everyone froze.

"I'm sorry for this, sir," spoke a lean man with a high forehead as he stood beside the stallions' glistening coats. His dark suit wrapped around his shoulders while his small eyes held steady on Ju-han. "I assure you, you will be compensated for your trial and you have my word: this will never happen again. I am the hotel manager, Han Moon-shin, and I sincerely apologize for all of this."

Ju-han's eyebrows, scowling high on his forehead in anger, slowly descended and his shoulders relaxed while he adjusted his black suit jacket. The hotel employees released him and stepped back.

"You seem to be a man of reason," Ju-han spoke at last. "I trust you will take care of things." He looked up and forced a smile while fastening the buttons of his coat.

"Yes, sir. Don't trouble yourself anymore about it." Moon-shin turned to the bellhops. "Gentlemen, unload the luggage for these fine people and let's make sure they are treated properly. And Mr. Lee!" he called to another dark-suited man nearby. "Deal with this driver, if you will," he waved at the shrunken man still trembling beside the carriage.

The manager motioned to Ju-han and Un-hee. "Follow me, please," he said.

Ju-han gripped Un-hee's elbow and they followed the slim man towards the doors yawning from the hotel's stone face. A golden light spilled from inside and warmed Un-hee's eyes; three chandeliers, choked from the ceiling by silver loops and dripping with crystal, bathed the lobby and hall beyond in a yellow wash. From the main entrance, she could see the front desk stretching beneath one of the chandeliers while its mahogany coat soaked in the very aroma of light. Even the creamy marble floors and pillars shone with a golden glow.

Un-hee stared in amazement at the rich interior. She had never seen such opulence in all her life and it overwhelmed her senses. Though she had desperately tried to keep step with Ju-han while they crossed the courtyard from the carriage, she was in awe at the magnificence before her and couldn't help pausing at the lobby entry.

Ju-han stopped next to her still clenching her arm. "What's wrong?" he asked.

"I don't fit here," she whispered slowly, her eyes moving through the hotel's interior. Behind the front desk, two giant banners swung side by side between granite pillars. The first one, in navy blue characters, invited everyone to enjoy the grand opening of the Sunrise Hotel during the first month of operation, August 1953. The second banner, carrying scarlet lettering painted over white, announced the victorious end of the Korean War and praise for the Great Republic of South Korea. Below the banners, long buffet tables scattered throughout the golden hall buckled under myriad varieties of seafood, vegetable, and pork dishes, rice, kimchi, and piled heaps of renowned Jeju oranges. Crowds of people thronged the area sending a blend of music, song and conversation flowing past Un-hee and Ju-han into the gathering night outside.

"You don't fit here?" Ju-han fumed at her.

Un-hee averted her eyes and remained silent.

"Yesterday, that would have been correct. But today, I'm quite sure you do. My family put down a lot of money for us to spend our first married week here, the most prestigious hotel on the entire island. Trust me, my bride: this is your life now. You fit here." Ju-han forced her forward with a squeeze of her arm.

Manager Han was standing beside the desk when they approached. "Please, check in and enjoy the food and festivities free of charge as long as you stay." Bowing slightly, his thin face split with a smile. "Again, I apologize for any inconvenience you experienced when arriving and I hope we will be able to serve you properly for the duration of your visit. I must excuse myself now as I have pressing matters to attend. Enjoy." He bowed once more and left them at the desk to join the crowds beyond in the hall.

"Welcome to the Sunrise Hotel," smiled a clerk with shiny black hair and a plump face. A pair of round glasses centered over his nose while he busied himself behind the reception desk.

"Thank you," replied Ju-han.

"I understand you had a wild ride down to the hotel?" He leaned forward and his eyes shone with interest. Un-hee looked down at the black nametag pinned to his wine-coloured vest. In white letters, it read "Kwan Jung-lee".

"You might say that," Ju-han glared in return. "Can we get on with this?"

Jung-lee immediately dropped his gaze and shuffled through some papers in front of him. "I have your reservation completed right here," he stammered, pushing his glasses farther up his nose. "All we need from you are your signatures in our official guest book. It will be a lasting record of everyone who helped us celebrate our grand opening." The clerk motioned to the end of the counter where a book bound in leather laid open, revealing pages edged with gold. A feather pen stood in a bottle next to the book.

Jung-lee offered Un-hee the inked quill and she quickly stroked her name into history. Following her, Ju-han signed his name on the line below. As he stood back to examine his writing, he saw how his name sat on the line under his wife's and his cheeks flushed with shame. In a flurry, he scratched her name from the roll and threw the quill onto the book.

"Sign again," he commanded, and softly she penned her name once more, this time under his as she steadied her trembling left hand against the book's thick cover. When she had finished, she nodded shyly at Jung-lee and replaced the feathered quill.

Without hesitation, Ju-han gripped her elbow and led her around the desk toward the center throng of guests. The feast shook with the rhythm of celebration: brash music with warbled singing blared from all directions, competing with the din of hundreds of conversations. On the buffet tables, a splendour unmatched filled Un-hee's eyes; she had never seen so much food in her entire life. Black tuxedos, stiff army uniforms, and colourful hanboks all swirled the tables and the neighbouring hall into a sea of festivity.

Waiters carrying drinks weaved through the crowd, and Ju-han was already onto his second glass of soju before they reached the first table. "The liquor flows like water in here," he smiled at Un-hee, one hand still twisting her elbow in its vise. She watched the separation between his front teeth, thinking it seemed wider to her than before.

They found the edge of the table where Un-hee sampled some spicy octopus spread on a silver platter. "Don't have too much, my bride. You wouldn't want to spoil your appetite for later, would you?" winked Ju-han, draining the bottom of a third glass.

Suddenly, he released her arm as a man in military green shook him from behind. "If I wasn't so polite, I'd be insulted!" the man blared, the loose flesh on his neck and face jiggling as he spoke. His glassy eyes strayed back and forth behind large, square bifocals while his oily skin glistened under the chandeliers.

"Who are you?" growled Ju-han, stepping back from the man's bulging stomach and probing hands. His jacket sparkled with multi-coloured war medals.

The man leaned his face towards Un-hee's as his eyes roamed about, trying to focus on hers. "You'd think he'd remember his favourite commanding officer?" he breathed in mock indignance.

His words slurred together and his lisp made it even more difficult for Un-hee to understand him. When an alcohol-tainted shroud struck her face a moment later, she couldn't mask her disgust.

"Especially since he saved my life!" the man continued. His eyelids stretched open their widest as his face swung back to Ju-han.

"Colonel Cho! How incredible!" exclaimed Ju-han as he jumped forward and hugged the beefy man.

"Now that's better! I was wondering when you'd come around," Cho shook in reply. He held Ju-han by the shoulders and smiled, displaying a mouthful of silver dental work.

"I'm sorry, Colonel. But you can't load me with all the blame here. The last time I saw you, you looked more like a tree than a man in those mountains north of Seoul." Ju-han took in the full appearance of the Colonel. "You look much... healthier now."

"And I feel better too, my son. The soju has warmed my heart and the end of the war has warmed my soul. It's a wonderful day for Korea. We stand on the threshold and look to a

61

prosperous new horizon. You were there, Ju-han. You are a walking witness to our bitter history. Those were days filled with terror and nights of fear. But we have prevailed, and victory is ours. Our people have proved to be strong and resilient, and not easily defeated." His voice began to quiver as he straightened his back and hoisted his decorated shoulders. "Our nation has endured dark years of tyranny, oppression, and occupation. Our women were tortured and our young men were killed. Yet the Korean people refused to be broken, and today we can breathe free air because our nation never surrendered."

Colonel Cho set his wine glass down on the table, removed his spectacles and wiped his lips and face with a handkerchief. Then his hands tightened into fists and he looked over Ju-han to the end of the hall, his moist eyes glimmering with tears. "It's a shame you weren't with us in those final days, Ju-han."

"That was not my choice to make, Colonel. My father wished a different future for me, one outside the military."

"Such a dutiful son," the Colonel admired, patting Ju-han on the cheek. "And such a skilled soldier. How I wish that Korea had more young men like you. Her shores would be forever safe. But now Ju-han," the Colonel slurred, replacing his bifocals and turning his glassy gaze towards Un-hee. "Who is this vision who stands beside you?"

Un-hee again smelled the reek of his breath. As she stared into his empty, silver-plated mouth, she felt a fist clutch her heart and tighten around it while air emptied from her lungs.

"This is my lovely new bride, Park Un-hee," Ju-han beamed. "We were married just today in Jeju City, and we're here for our honeymoon."

"I am in awe in your presence, Park Un-hee. You are radiant."

Un-hee bowed and smiled as politely as she could, but she still could force no breath into her chest. Colonel Cho swayed as he looked into her eyes, and then wavered back towards her husband. "Ju-han, you have laid claim to a rare jewel here. Long may you live in wedded harmony," he grinned, his chrome teeth glinting in the light.

"Thank you, Colonel."

"Come now, my young doves. Let me show you the finer points of this feast. The table laid before you has been many years in waiting."

Cho led Ju-han and Un-hee through the throngs of people to the west hall, and the young bride struggled to keep pace with her husband as he seized her arm and pulled her past crowds of dignitaries and high-ranking army officers. The dazzling costumes and colours spinning by mirrored her descent down a road not of her choosing. The opulence, decadence, and luxury that confronted her were foreign elements and dangerous to the eyes of a peasant farmer's daughter. Her young life had taught her the value of the soil; how it sustains everyone, from the greatest to the small. Because of her humble childhood, she saw dignity in her father's bent back, in her grandmother's gnarled hands and worn face, and her legs bowed from years of toil. She knew the worth of work, to such a degree that she had wished nothing more than to marry Shin-char and till the land together for their provision to the end of their allotted days.

But the stream of her life had chosen a different course to follow. Here, in an elegant hotel ballroom, she was surrounded by more harvest from the land than she had ever seen. And Un-hee knew that the guests feeding freely had probably never pulled even a single onion from the ground with their own hands. As she spun through the intoxicated crowd, she sensed a loathing for these elitists, and knew she should loathe herself as well, since she now belonged within their sphere.

They arrived at the entrance to the cavernous west hall, where towering ceilings framed with wooden arches looked down upon a dim room lit only by torches on the walls and candles on the tables. The food was less abundant here, but liquor coursed like a river: wine casks, beer kegs, and soju bottles outnumbered the guests in the hall.

"Now this is a celebration worthy of the occasion," praised Cho, lifting his arms to the dark reaches above him.

"And you, Colonel, are a true guide," applauded Ju-han, reaching for a glass of wine. "We'll drink to your bravery that has bought our peace."

Colonel Cho's face sobered suddenly. "My son, it was the thousands of young Korean men who paid for our peace with their blood. This is to their honour and memory." He and Ju-han emptied their glasses simultaneously.

"Here, my bride, are the true fruits of freedom," Ju-han grinned broadly over his shoulder at Un-hee between gulps. "Come and taste!"

The trio moved slowly through the hall, the men proceeding with patience whenever they came across a new kind of alcohol. Un-hee watched and quietly worried as her husband became drunk before her eyes. He rarely remembered to hold her arm anymore but she feared the liquor in his veins would feed his temper, and the unseen clutch upon her heart tightened still more as she trembled at the loud banter passing between the two men.

She wanted to flee, to vanish. As a child, Un-hee had seen the fearful effects of alcohol through the bonds it wrapped around her father. By day, he was a stern, hard-working man with a quiet mouth and strong hands. But by the time the moon had lifted its bleak face over the fields of rice, he was an entirely different animal, at times raging, at times sullen, and almost always abusive. Very early, Un-hee had learned to deal with her father's transformations: she had learned to run, physically when she could, mentally when she was trapped. She had fled from him her entire life, and had distanced herself even more after the Japanese took her mother and illness claimed her grandmother; now she would have to flee from his choice of a husband as well.

Un-hee had known this marriage was a mistake from the beginning and, but for her father, never would have entered into it. Later, she had decided to endure it for the sake of her family, to preserve the honour of their name. However, from the hour this day had begun, she had known she could never live the rest of her life shackled to this man. Yesterday, she had feared and hated his family; tonight, she feared and hated him. She had no choice but to flee again: from Ju-han, from the hotel, from her entire life. But how? Her fears poured in upon her from all directions.

"My husband?" she whispered, touching Ju-han's shoulder lightly.

"Yes?" he replied, swinging around from the table with a glass in each hand.

"I have to use the bathroom. I'll be right back." She shone forth her best smile and tried to appear content and relaxed.

Ju-han set a glass down and studied her face for several moments while stroking the back of her neck. "Sure," he answered, appearing convinced. "Don't be long."

five

"Quite a historic time for marriage…" Un-hee heard the Colonel's voice trail off as she stepped through the crowd towards the restrooms. She pushed open the metal door and walked over to the sinks. The bathroom glittered everywhere with new chrome and tile, more elegant than anything Un-hee had ever witnessed.

As she looked in the mirror, her reflection stared back in amazement. Her hair was pinned up high on her head and her face was glowing. She had forgotten how beautiful her hanbok was, and how much she looked like her mother from her wedding photo. In an instant, her mind flashed through her childhood dreams of marriage and the years she had spent with Shin-char before the war began. How perfect everything would be, she thought, if he were the man waiting for me outside right now. And for a fleeting moment, her heart was able to rise from beneath the chains that ensnared it, and beat freely within her. She had never known another love, and his strong arms and gentle touch had been with her through many trials. But he was gone forever, and she was married to another. When she again looked deep into her eyes, the chains fell heavy once more and she knew what had been grinding against the fabric of her soul these past few months: she could never live without love.

Her gaze dropped and rested on the jeweled necklace hanging about her neck. Ju-han's father had presented it to her just that morning as a gift before the wedding ceremony, and he had fastened it himself. His loud lips had praised her beauty, and what a stunning couple her and Ju-han made. He had told her how thrilled he was that she would now be part of the family and he anticipated the many warm moments they would all share together.

Un-hee had been unable to look at him, however, for when she saw his eyes, her mother's eyes cried out to her, and when she glanced down, her mother's blood covered his hands. She had begun to tremble in front of him with fear and anger and grief while a sickening dread had covered her heart, but she had hidden it all under an excited laugh and an excuse of nervousness. Now, as her own eyes stared into the mirror, she saw that a sparkling noose was clasped around her throat.

I will escape this caged union, she vowed. I will escape right now.

Un-hee turned from the mirror and walked back to the steel door. She eased it open and peeked through the guests towards the west wing. The milling crowd and dim hall made it impossible to see if Ju-han and the Colonel were still there, but the throng of people filling the floor between her and the men made Un-hee confident she could slip away undetected in the opposite direction and head towards the front lobby. There, maybe she would be able to beg the hotel staff to hide her until she could escape.

Slowly, she slid through the doorway, still keeping her gaze on the dark hall across the room. She could see neither of the two men, so she was satisfied they couldn't see her. She turned towards the lobby, but stiffened on her first step. Directly in front of her was Colonel Cho, leaning on the wall with his back towards her! His wide shoulders under the green army uniform filled her vision while the back of his head revealed a bald crown covered by hair pulled over from the side of his head. Un-hee could now hear his lisping words slurring together, which before had slipped by her unnoticed while her attention was on the west hall.

"… so your father wrote a letter saying that if it was within my reach, if I could possibly move him to the heaviest offensive position." The Colonel's hand clutched a wine glass as it swung out towards the crowd. Un-hee shrank against the wall.

"Really? I had no idea," Ju-han's voice responded from somewhere in front of the Colonel. Un-hee began slipping back along the wall towards the bathroom door.

"I felt it my duty to oblige considering your father's rank and history, but I never intended for the lad to die. He was one of five soldiers that were ambushed…" His voice stopped mid-sentence just as Un-hee felt the door with her left hand and pushed into it. She stood breathless inside the bathroom as the metal gate swung closed.

Suddenly, a hand shot out and stopped it with a dead thud just before it had fully shut.

"And here is your beautiful bride!" the Colonel beamed, swinging the door open again.

Ju-han appeared next to him in the doorway. "Are you about finished in there?"

"Yes," Un-hee replied, composing herself. "I was just on my way out to find you."

"The kind Colonel here has arranged a surprise for us and we came to see if you were done." Un-hee saw that Ju-han's face was now flush with wine. His cheeks burned and his eyes were misty.

"That's right, my newly-married. Come with me."

Colonel Cho led the way through the crowd again as Ju-han followed with a pinching grip on Un-hee's elbow.

"I saw you go back in there, woman!" Ju-han seethed as they kept pace behind the Colonel. "Why did you come out and go back in? Are you trying to avoid me?" The reek of alcohol descended on Un-hee through Ju-han's gritted teeth.

"No, no, of course not," she whispered in return. The hold upon her arm tightened. "I thought I forgot my lipstick, that's all."

"And did you?"

"No, I've got it right here inside my hanbok," Un-hee replied, patting the folds of her dress.

"That's good," Ju-han continued in a low growl. "Because if you did try to avoid or escape me, you know you would pay dearly for it."

Un-hee couldn't stifle a wince under his crushing grip on her arm.

"And here we are, my little songbirds." Cho spun around with his arms open and faced the couple. They had crossed the length of the banquet hall to the east end. "The hotel has hired a photographer to take pictures of all the dignitaries and officials here tonight. I have arranged for him to snap your portrait and record on film your happiest day."

A large fountain of pink and red marble sang behind the Colonel, the melting colours swirling together as in a bowl of ice cream. The walls of the basin were carved into waves that crashed amid clouds of foam while in the middle, three leaping fish spewed plumes of water into the air, which returned to the fountain as a constant shower. Behind it, tall windows looked out into the dark night beyond.

A balding man approached them, indicating that he was the photographer. "You make a very beautiful couple. Now that I have seen you, I agree with the Colonel here: this night would not be complete without your picture."

"That's very kind of you, thank you," grinned Ju-han.

"Please, take your places before the fountain," he directed while returning to his camera near the windows. The Colonel stood behind him and watched him work.

Just as the photographer was training his focus upon the couple, a whip of lightning lashed from the sky, followed closely by a deafening crack of thunder.

"Looks like a storm is coming to spend the night," the photographer mused as Un-hee shuddered from the powerful rumble.

Ju-han let go of her elbow and wrapped his arm around her back. "Do try to look happy for this photo, my bride. It might hang by the front desk welcoming guests to this hotel for many years to come. You wouldn't want to disappoint, would you?" He pulled her to his side with an iron clutch as he adjusted his suit jacket with his free hand.

"What a perfect couple," the photographer admired to the Colonel as he finished his final adjustments. He approached Un-hee and straightened the white bow on her hanbok. "You look like a melting cap of snow in front of a crimson tower," he admired, pulling at the hem of her dress to display all the pleats.

Un-hee smiled shyly at him, her head bowed.

Noticing Ju-han's stare, the photographer added, "And your husband is a chiseled pillar beside you. Let your personalities mesh before my lens and I will paint you."

He returned to his camera and together, he and the Colonel counted to three. The flash bulb ignited the scene, capturing Un-hee's warm smile next to Ju-han's smug grin.

The photographer bowed low. "Thank you greatly. I wish you a very happy honeymoon in paradise, and a story book life with each other." Un-hee and Ju-han bowed in acknowledgement.

"Now that was perfect," admired Cho, striding up to them with unsteady steps. His jowls shook again, "Just perfect."

"Thank you for arranging it for us, Colonel. That was thoughtful of you," Ju-han replied.

"You're welcome, my son. You've been dear to my heart, these past few years. I've thought of you often, and I've wondered what has become of you. You know, I began to worry," the Colonel started but then coughed and rested his hand on Ju-han's shoulder for support. "I began to worry when I heard those stories circulating about your father. I didn't want to believe them but..."

Ju-han stopped him short. "What stories? What are you talking about?"

Un-hee listened intently as she looked from her husband to Cho.

The Colonel's misty eyes looked puzzled as he gazed at Ju-han for a moment, and then at Un-hee. "Oh," he chuckled, a deep, watery laugh. "These are not issues to discuss before women, and much less at a party." He patted Ju-han's shoulder and turned toward the banquet tables. "I feel a thirst coming on. Why don't you two come join me in the west hall again?"

Ju-han was about to follow but then stopped. "Sorry, Colonel. We should get to our room before the storm hits. We're staying in the honeymoon suite behind the hotel."

Un-hee watched Ju-han's face and saw a flicker of resentment beneath the liquored exterior.

"Of course, that's fine, soldier. I wish you both a wonderful honeymoon," the Colonel shouted, swaying backwards while waving a hand in the air. He continued to mumble to himself as he swung around in the direction of the darkened hall.

"I'm not at all tired yet," Un-hee murmured as they watched the Colonel wade into the crowd. "You could go with him if you wanted to."

"Don't tell me what I can do," Ju-han snarled, his face burnt and scowling. "You are coming with me and we are going to our room now!" His fingered vise closed once more around Un-hee's elbow and led her to the front lobby.

Jung-lee was sorting through some papers at the reception desk when they arrived. "Has our luggage been brought to our suite yet?" demanded Ju-han.

"Yes, Mr. Kim," replied the clerk, pushing his glasses furiously up his nose. "It was taken immediately when you checked in. Would you like to see the suite now?"

At the nod of Ju-han's head, Jung-lee motioned for a bellhop to join him and they directed Un-hee and Ju-han across the festive hall to the glass doors beyond. These opened onto the lawn behind the hotel. A sidewalk of smooth lava rock stretched out into the night while yellow globes, perched atop posts on either side, spilled their light onto the path. Sparsely scattered palm trees throughout the grounds tossed their black leaves in the gathering wind far above while a carpet of grass reached from the rear of the hotel to the cliff's lip and looked down upon the roaring surf below.

A warm wind swept over Un-hee as she followed the guides. The stony trail led to the center of the lawn where a guesthouse stood with darkened windows. Its hood and walls of rock complimented the castle air of the hotel while its double glass doors swung open towards the ocean. As she reached the entrance, Un-hee felt the first great drops from the shifting heavens splash down upon her neck, and when she looked back, she saw lightning spark from behind dark clouds out over the ocean. Following Ju-han into the suite, she shuddered as the accompanying thunder, spilling down from the sky, rattled the doors and windows.

Inside, the newly wedded pair followed the stewards closely, listening to Jung-lee chatter nervously and watching him adjust his glasses as he explained the various features of the suite: a king size bed, a bathroom fashioned from polished granite, and a jetted tub hidden under a large window facing the blackness beyond the cliffs. The guesthouse was self-contained and equipped with every possible luxury.

"The windows," the clerk explained, "are wonderful. They are soundproof, so you won't be bothered by any outside noise, except maybe the thunder that's rolling towards us tonight, and they are tinted and mirrored, so no one can see in day or night. You'll have privacy beyond measure."

Un-hee glanced at the large pane facing the sea. The rain was beginning to weep on the glass as sudden shards of light pierced through the ink outside.

The guides stopped in front of the doors upon completing their task. "We wish to congratulate you both on being the first couple ever to enjoy the splendour of the Sunrise Hotel honeymoon suite," Jung-lee smiled, his round face breathless. "For your convenience and pleasure, there is no communication from the hotel to the guesthouse. That phone," he pointed at the black telephone near the bed, "is for outbound calls only. This way, there will be no interruptions from hotel staff, other guests, or the outside world; you are completely secluded."

The clerks both announced, "Have a wonderful stay!" in unison as they bowed.

When Jung-lee glanced up again, Un-hee's stricken stare met his eyes from where she stood behind Ju-han. For the briefest moment, the clerk returned her gaze with a puzzled look but quickly mastered his curiosity and reprised his role of subordinate.

But the exchanged had not passed unnoticed. Immediately, Ju-han's eyes whipped back to see what had attracted the clerk's attention and there, beside the bed, stood Un-hee, head bowed and hands folded in front of her. Ju-han waved for the stewards to depart. A peal of thunder burst in with a gush of rain as they closed the doors behind them.

"What just happened there?" demanded Ju-han.

"Where?" Un-hee wondered, sitting down on the bed. She looked up wearing her most genuinely confused expression.

"Do not take me for a fool, woman! That would be your last mistake," roared Ju-han, rushing forward and thrusting his finger under Un-hee's chin, craning it up towards him. "The boy saw something behind me, and you were all it could have been. What were you doing?"

Un-hee slowly slid away along the edge of the bed and let her eyes fall back to the floor. "I was merely listening to them. Then I adjusted my headpiece and bow. I have no idea what you are talking about."

"Well, I suppose it doesn't matter anyway," Ju-han softened his voice and sat down next to her. He rubbed his hand down her cheek, curled it beneath her chin, and then placed a finger on her lips. "Now you are mine, and so you will always be."

Un-hee bridged the space between them with a gaze of indifference. She noticed this was the first time he had touched her that she had not shivered. She looked directly into his black eyes, and there saw frailty and a smallness that had eluded her until now. She had always looked at him through her knowledge of the past, through the foul deeds of his father. But as she saw Ju-han at this moment, within his drunken eyelids she glimpsed a coward who always struck first because he was unable to defend himself; behind his misty pupils, she saw a boy peering out from the body of a man; inside those angry eyes, she saw fear wrapped in a proud shadow.

"I need to change. I'm exhausted," Un-hee sighed, rising several moments later.

"That's a good idea," said Ju-han, lying down on the bed with his hands folded behind his head. "I'll be waiting."

Un-hee carried her suitcase to the bathroom and locked the door as quietly as she could. She began taking the hairpiece out of her hair while her mind tumbled ever faster about what she should do. She loathed the idea of sleeping with Ju-han, and she knew she could never bear it, even for a single night, yet escape from him was impossible. He held the keys to her life now. She was trapped in a cage guarded from the inside by her husband, her only true hate. She blinked through several fresh tears, seeing the face of her despair looking back at her in the mirror.

Slipping out of her hanbok, she hung it on a hook behind the door and cinched the bow tight, admiring the fabric. She draped her headpiece over it, and then climbed into a set of white silk pajamas, also given to her by Ju-han's family. From her suitcase, Un-hee pulled a flat package and unraveled the leather cord that held the fabric bound. With the cloth laid open, she picked through some personal papers until she found a letter wrapped around a worn photograph of her mother and her grandmother. Pulling the picture out, she gazed into the women's simmering eyes that blistered from the picture, and she remembered her grandma's weathered face and mouth that used to chide her as a child. She looked down and thought of the hard hands that had administered her mother's strict discipline upon her during childhood, and she longed to feel their coarseness again. Kissing the photo, Un-hee tucked it into an inner pocket of her nightshirt.

Next, she opened the letter and carefully straightened its creases on the counter. As she began to read over the lines she had known by heart for months, she tenderly sounded each word in her head.

To my beautiful Un-hee,   *Feb.22, 1953*

I long to be with you, my sweet! My eyes are blind without you and my heart bursts for the day that I can see you and hold you in my arms again. I ache for you, my love. You are life to me, and I know that without you, I cannot live. I know I told you my duty was supposed to finish this week but they have re-assigned me. We are going to be part of...

She paused. She could hear a hand on the doorknob. The gold ball turned slowly, but then stopped.

"Why is this locked?" Ju-han's roar came through the door as he pounded on it. "What's taking you so long?"

"I'll be done in a second." Un-hee quickly swept the letters and cloth off the counter and into the open suitcase, which she folded up and set beside the bathtub. Glancing in the mirror, she quickly wiped her eyes, and pushed back her hair.

The instant she unlocked the door, she was thrown backwards onto the floor as Ju-han rushed in. He looked like a crazed bull, his eyes flaming from their sockets. He picked her up, sat her on the counter beside the sink, and began violently kissing her. Un-hee gagged as his body reeked of liquor and his mouth tasted bitter and sticky. She was pressed up against the mirror and still he continued pushing forward, holding both her arms behind her. Finally, she was able to dig her heels into his hips and kick him back.

"What are you doing?" she stammered, gasping for breath.

"You are my bride. I will have you," he answered, moving forward again.

"Not like that, you won't!" replied Un-hee, lifting up her heels again. "If you consider me your bride, you'll treat me with respect."

"Respect?" he laughed, his eyebrows glaring higher on his forehead. "For a poor farmer's daughter? I'm sure that'll never happen. You know, I've been thinking about all that has happened today and it's actually working out rather well except for one thing: you still need to be taught to fear. You should be a little more terrified of me than you are right now. The fact that you're not makes me think that you don't quite understand your role yet, or my power."

"I understand that you are not worthy or capable of love."

Ju-han stepped forward so that he was draped over Un-hee's knees and his nose nearly touched hers. His alcohol breath made her feel like gagging once more. "It's just as my daddy said. Women need to be broken and trained and then they will serve well."

Un-hee held his drunken gaze. "Your dad was a dog, which makes you a puppy, I guess."

"Now that was clever, just wait till you hear me growl."

"You know, I don't care what you do," she said, pushing him back with her heels again. "Just don't talk to me about your dad."

"Why not? He's more rich and important than your dad could ever dream to be."

"You don't know much about him, do you?"

Ju-han was visibly startled at the question. "What could you know that I don't?"

"Your father is a traitor to Korea, Ju-han. Did you know that? Your father sent Korean women to the Japanese army to be raped and tortured and killed; did you know that?" Un-hee was bursting inside and could not hold back the waves of tears within her as she thought of the wicked man who had given her the necklace just that morning. "Your father betrayed this country. Your family is rich because your father sold Korean women's lives! My mother's life! Did you know that?"

Ju-han leapt forward and caught Un-hee by the throat. She neither flinched nor shifted her teary eyes from his. "You lie, woman. You lie, and I will make you pay for your lies," he seethed through clenched teeth. He released her neck and began pacing the bathroom floor.

Un-hee wiped the tears from her cheeks and, as she watched Ju-han walk back and forth, she no longer felt any fear in his presence, only loathing. She saw a small, drunken shell of a man striding in front of her. "You're not half the man my true fiancée was. That's why you had to force me to marry you. Nobody else would."

Ju-han stopped and adjusted his suit jacket. He took a deep breath and looked over at Un-hee. "You don't know how near the mark you touch."

"What do you mean?"

"Your 'true' fiancée, his name was Byun Shin-char, right?"

"Yes," she answered, stunned.

"Just some poor farm shit, I would imagine," he laughed to himself. "He was killed in the war, wasn't he?"

Un-hee nodded her head silently as she cursed herself for bringing Shin-char's name up. She kept her eyes steady on Ju-han as she struggled to hold back the torrent of memories that swelled within her heart, ready to wash over her.

"Yes, I think I've heard of him," continued Ju-han, again pacing up and down the bathroom floor. "It's kind of an intriguing story, isn't it? I believe he was nearly finished his war duty when he was suddenly called up on another mission, one that dealt him a fatal wound. And wasn't he secretly betrothed to you? How unfortunate, what an ill fate!"

Ju-han stopped and stared at her in mock surprise. "Now, let's see if all this makes sense: had he made it home, he would have sought your hand in marriage, the very hand that had already been openly promised to me by your father. A woman with two lovers, now that sounds very scandalous. What would you have done if I had not stepped in to help? It seems you are actually indebted to me for saving you from such an undesirable predicament."

"How could you possibly know all that?"

"Someone always knows. It's just a matter of finding the right person at the right time to narrow the options, and then one hand washes the other."

"What are you saying, that Shin-char's death was intentional?" She paused for several seconds as his words began to make perfect sense in her mind with the final events of Shin-char's life. "You filthy dog, you had him killed!"

Un-hee buried her face in her knees upon the counter where she was curled up. She fought for control over her emotions. She desperately wanted to show Ju-han nothing of herself, but her heart ached to be with Shin-char, and the wounds of her loss were yet so tender and fresh.

"Please, don't assume to know. I had nothing to do with it. Actually, I only found out about the whole thing tonight. I was just showing you how worthy I am of your gratitude by saving you from disgrace." His tone reeked of superiority and, despite knowing that he was trying to enrage her, Un-hee desired to lash out at him. She shook with pain and rage for several moments, desperately trying to bury Shin-char's memory within her. Soon, she was sitting motionless, her head still bowed.

"Come to bed, Un-hee," Ju-han pulled on her arm.

"Don't touch me," replied Un-hee in a cold monotone, and then jerked her arm away from him.

Seeing her defiance ignited Ju-han's black eyes with a chilling light. "You, my bride, will do as I say."

He reached for her throat and tore the necklace away that still sparkled around her neck. "This you will wear when you are worthy!" he spat as he threw it on the floor. Then he seized her by the shoulders and hauled her off the counter.

Holding both her arms firmly in front of him, he pushed her backwards from the bathroom. She kicked at him and resisted as much as she could but she was no match. His strength far surpassed hers, and his anger was fueled by liquor, which created a lethal poison within him.

He dragged her to the bed and threw her onto it. Un-hee scrambled over the other side but Ju-han was too fast. He leapt onto her and had her pinned beneath him before she could get away.

"Now I have you, my precious bride," he smirked as he pushed her hair back from her face. "You were bought with a high price and I intend to get my money's worth!"

He pulled his arms out of the tuxedo jacket and threw it on the floor. Just as he started ripping at the buttons on his dress shirt, a fantastic spear of lightning blazed through the night and lit the interior of the suite with white fire. In that moment, all the lamps inside the guesthouse extinguished, plunging Un-hee and Ju-han into a murky dusk lit only by the warm glow of the hotel melting through the windows.

"What perfect atmosphere," chuckled Ju-han, continuing to tear at his shirt while thunder drummed against the walls.

Un-hee looked up at the evil grin leering down at her in the dirty yellow half-light. "Ju-han, please. Don't do this, not this way!" she begged, her arms aching under his knees.

"My little sparrow! What a different song you sing now than the one you were chirping in the bathroom!" He pulled his dress shirt over his head, revealing a tattooed chest. "You seem to play the game quite well," he grinned. "Your resistance is very appealing."

"This is a terrible sin you are committing! Ju-han, look at me!" Un-hee's eyes were so piercing and her voice so troubled that Ju-han ceased undressing. "Stop now, or you will pay greatly for this."

Ju-han stared unblinking for some seconds at Un-hee's pleading face before his glassy gaze returned and soft laughter escaped his lips. He slowly pulled his belt out from around his waist and tossed it to the ground.

"I will have what's mine, bride. You need to learn your place in the world, and I'll be happy to show you."

Beyond the tear-streaked window, rain had started to plunge down from the heavens in a steady torrent, soaking the lawn and shimmering palm trees. Every few minutes, lightning would slash a brilliant wound across the cloak of night, which the darkness would sew up immediately. And following close behind the stitching was the clamour of mighty stones striking one another as they fell from the belly of the storm. Inside the hotel's elegant lobby, the celebration extended far into the night; guests continued to dance and drink, eat and talk, and laugh at the rumbles of thunder as the muted screams of a bride's distress rose only to the wind and the rain.

six

She lay on her side. Behind her, Ju-han's arm draped over her shoulder and held her prisoner as he slept. Un-hee withered on the bed like a flower left in the blazing sun, like a bruised rose that had been trampled over and ripped out by the roots. Her eyes were stuck wide. Her soul hung in torn ribbons, and her heart wept inside a hollow ribcage. She felt a fire between her legs that she wished would flare up and consume her entire body, leaving Ju-han to awaken next to a charred corpse. She longed for her bones to become fuel and torch in the furnace of her skin. She wanted her burnt flesh to be a stench in his nostrils that would torment him to madness for the rest of his existence.

Un-hee loathed him more now than she ever thought possible, and she knew that her options had narrowed: flight or murder. She couldn't begin to decide what she would need in order to kill Ju-han, so she settled on escaping from him, tonight, now. His presence spread through her like a disease, and every sickening moment near him made her more determined to leave. His breath was hot and clammy on the back of her neck, and one of his feet had pushed its way in between her ankles. His arm lay like lead upon her shoulder, as though it were slowly crushing her chest, and every place his body touched hers, Un-hee sensed his malice flowing.

Slowly, she moved her top foot, then her bottom one, away from his intruding leg. She slid her feet over, so that now they dangled above the floor off the side of the bed. He groaned quietly and curled his legs away from her body. Ever so slightly, she budged his arm up her shoulder to drape it across the side of her neck, its sticky heat melting into her skin. Next, she moved her pillow down beside her face and rested his hand on it. In this way, she was finally able to slide her head out from underneath by propping his arm up on the pillow.

Gingerly, she placed her feet on the floor and sat for a minute on the edge of the bed, making sure he was still soundly asleep. She looked back and saw his mouth gaping and his breath passing in rhythm as he exhaled heavily. And as she watched his eyelids clench stiffly together and then ease, she marveled how even in sleep his eyebrows curled upwards in a grimace.

As a moving statue, she gradually rose from the bed and stepped lightly across the empty floor to the bathroom, though the ground was firm and suffered no sound to escape it. Once she had pulled the door wide enough, she slipped into the gloom and retrieved her suitcase, still leaning against the bathtub. To Un-hee, a seeming eternity passed before she had it completely shut, each noisy tooth in the zipper track attempting to betray her with sound.

She looked around at the soap, shampoo and cologne spilled on the floor next to the tub while Ju-han's assault played through her mind again.

In a fraction of a moment, she questioned the unbalance of power that had dominated her world thus far, and wondered if Ju-han would ever be repaid for his cruelty. And what about his father? Would he ever learn and endure the same torment to which he sent her mother, along with innumerable other Korean women? As she straightened, Un-hee saw her dark reflection in the mirror: pain etched the glass with a diamond-shaped tear as her reflection smeared together with the black shower curtain behind her.

Her bare feet skipped softly to the door and she peeked around the corner towards the bed. In the muddy light, she could see Ju-han still lying on his side with his arms reaching across the bed towards her. From a lightning bolt's momentary snapshot, she saw that his eyes remained closed while his mouth yet gaped; so, patiently, she crossed the room, keeping step with the rolling thunder until she attained the front doors. Her hand sat ready on the smooth doorknob and she was about to twist it to freedom when she stopped and stood motionless in the darkness. Her mind had arrested her escape with one question: where will you go? Indeed, to whom could she run and be safely hidden from Ju-han's claws?

As she leaned her head against the door, she could sense the obstacles that plagued her brain pressing hard upon the rain-soaked glass outside: her hotel room knelt beneath a torrential downpour; her only exit from the hotel grounds lay behind her through a guest-choked lobby; the road to her home wound many miles over the shoulder of a volcano and she had no money, no food, and no vehicle.

And even if she were to reach her home safely through all those snares, her father would undoubtedly send her straight back to Ju-han to preserve the family honour. Un-hee's devils, grim-faced and powerful, held vigil beyond the doors of that honeymoon suite, and she knew they guarded her misery. Yet behind her, on the bed, slept their captain and commanding officer. She knew she had no options left. She would choose the lesser evil. She would flee into the night.

Easing open the door, she stared into the mouth of darkness that yawned before her, spitting a sheet of rain into the room. She had just crossed the threshold when a spear of lightning shot from the sky followed by the roaring of an avalanche of stones. Un-hee's heart stopped as the clamour descended all around her. She spun back to look in the suite. There, in the middle of the bed, sat Ju-han's black shape staring straight at her!

Un-hee was paralyzed. Her skin froze and cracked. And in that moment, had the light allowed, it would have shown drops of rain streaking over her face and freezing into icy spheres.

The fear of retribution, fear for her life caused her to flee from those doors into that soaking night. In her shock, she had dropped her suitcase, and in her haste, she had not picked it up again.

Her silk pajamas fluttered behind her like a white banner as she sprinted towards the darkest area she could find, straight ahead. Behind her lay the hotel spilling its yellow light into the storm while directly before her stood the tall cliff whose roots bathed in the Pacific Ocean.

Un-hee screamed as she glanced back and saw a dark figure set against the golden brilliance of the hotel, running after her. She turned towards the ocean again and screamed a second time, though she could still hear no sound leaving her lips, only the fury of the storm. She tried to look ahead but the rain, sweeping in from the sea, stung her eyelids shut. When lightning struck, the trees ahead of her looked like platinum pillars with arms and fingers of silver, and when night closed in again, blackness filled her sight and she sprinted blind.

Suddenly, a railing appeared before her and she knew she was trapped. In front of her was the cliff edge that dropped all the way to the water while behind, the worst enemy she had ever known approached. She could think only of escaping him at all costs so she scrambled over the wooden railing where the sound of furious waves pounding rocky shores rose in chorus and filled her ears. She saw the black figure advancing towards her, each step slow and deliberate.

"Get away from me!" she screamed into the angry wind.

The figure stopped.

Several moments passed and then a voice rasped out of the darkness, "I'm only here to help you." As he replied, Ju-han took two more steps closer to the railing.

"If you want to help me then leave! You're the one forcing me over this cliff!" Un-hee shouted back. Though she gripped the railing with all her might, the wood was slimy with rain and her hands could scarcely keep her from falling.

"I love you, Un-hee. You are my bride, I didn't mean to hurt you. I promise I never will again." Ju-han reached out his hand towards Un-hee.

"I will never be your bride!"

At that moment, two streaks of lightning slashed from the sky and set silver daylight about them for an instant. Un-hee's eyes, wild with fear, saw a flash of Ju-han lunging towards her with both hands groping for her throat. His curled lips and bared teeth grinned as a wolf's at the rabbit caught in the trap. Un-hee let go of the railing and pushed off with her legs to escape. Ju-han's claws grasped only air as Un-hee sailed to the waves and rocks below, accompanying the cascading thunder that fell with her down the cliff face.

seven

Ju-han's waist hit the railing as he saw Un-hee fall just beyond his fingertips. He screamed after her and believed his throat would explode from the force he sent through it. As he watched her fluttering white form disappear into the depths below, he was convinced he was watching a movie screen because she fell so slowly and so silently before his eyes. He wondered why she didn't fall faster, and why he couldn't just reach out and touch her if she appeared so close.

After she was gone, he continued to stare into the abyss that had swallowed his bride and wondered when she would reappear. Seeing that she remained hidden, Ju-han raised one leg over the wooden barrier and was about to follow after her when he stopped. All of a sudden, he was aware of rain stinging his cheeks, and felt the violent wind threatening to tear his dress shirt from his body. The roar of the surf swelled in his ears and brief bursts of lightning showed him a cauldron far below, churning with waves. Fear filled him, and he turned around and climbed back over the railing, collapsing on the grass. Rain drenched his body as he lay with his arms and legs spread under the storm.

His mind reeled. His skin felt numb and chilled. For a moment, he thought he might have also died as bolts of light flashed above illuminating black, spiny fingers reaching over him. Death's terrible minions had come to claim their own, he thought. When he realized he was only looking up at the branches of the pine trees, his breathing quieted and he sensed a little warmth creep back into his body.

But disquiet soon emerged. Thinking about Un-hee plummeting to her ruin sickened his stomach and made him want to gag. He tried to rid the image from his brain but her plunging white shape remained before his eyes, whether they were open or closed. He thrashed his head from side to side, scratching at his hair and clawing nail marks into his brow to rid his mind of the memory. He screamed into the night at the height of his voice, and thought the branches above him swayed back from his fury, but still Un-hee's spinning form continued to fall away from him into darkness, and yet never grow smaller.

Ju-han desperately tried to shift his thoughts elsewhere but they remained cemented on his bride. Though he tried to stop it, the day and the night played back in his mind as he lay under the swirling fury of the wind. He twisted from the recollection, coiling his body in spasms and fits, and still the images persisted. He saw a meek and submissive woman, a beautiful woman. A woman he had relished to call his own. His bride belonged to him and she was supposed to like his advances; she was supposed to submit. Submit! He craved the word, and lusted after its effects. Now that he had shown his full power, she was to fear him and serve him for life, to submit to him.

He cried out again into the night. How could she have escaped him? How could she have rejected him, even to the death? He hated submission for he hated what it had brought him. He had never believed, even for a moment, that she would actually jump from that cliff. She was only a female; she lacked the will, the conviction. Within his brain, Ju-han couldn't wed such a weak woman to such defiant actions. He had done exactly what his father had taught him all his life, and now his bride was dead.

And yet here she was, fluttering before his eyes still. He could feel a hot hate growing in his chest as he watched her spin like a snowflake between the branches above him. Anger like he had never felt before, like a glowing plate of metal, flushed within him at the obstinate woman who had been his bride. His body shook and his muscles stiffened as rage continued to mount.

When he could no longer contain himself, Ju-han surged to his feet and marched back to the railing, kicking it with all his might. To his surprise, a meter-long section of fence broke off and tumbled over the cliff. Ju-han fell to the ground at the sudden collapse, his body sliding forward as his feet dangled in empty space. He spun onto his stomach and splayed out his arms, grasping for whatever his hands could reach, but everything felt wet and slippery. Sliding down even farther, he would have followed Un-hee's fate had the bushes trapped between his desperate fingers not arrested his fall.

By now, his feet and legs, all the way up to his waist, swayed in the darkness below the cliff's lip. The wind continued to tear in from the ocean and repeatedly dashed Ju-han's legs against the rock. He could hear the full power of the waves growling below as they punished the shoreline. Their strength terrified him and he realized he could draw no breath because his chest was crushed against the cliff's edge. He tried to hoist himself back up but the bushes, soaked with rain, slowly slipped through his hands and shed their leaves.

Finally, in one last burst, Ju-han kicked off the cliff and used the momentum to pull himself higher. Then he grasped for a new anchor and his hands closed around the broken stump of the railing still standing in the ground. He used it to pull himself up from the edge and crawl away to safety on the lawn. Crumpling onto his stomach, Ju-han lay without moving while his heart pounded into the earth. He could no longer feel the wind or the rain; he was only glad to be alive.

Spears of lightning stirred him from the soaked lawn long after his heart rate had returned to normal. He dragged himself to his knees and looked up at the castle beyond, each of its golden eyes watching him. He felt naked. The wind rushing past exposed him to those lamps, and he feared them. He was only one where there should have been two. His bride was gone from him, forever, and he had no credible tale to give for he could never tell anyone the truth.

The thunder pounding down around him shook his brain, and he realized he needed an alibi. A bride falls from a cliff on her wedding night in the middle of a storm with her husband a meter away. With no witnesses, they will undoubtedly think I killed her, he thought. I will face prison, or maybe even a death sentence. Ju-han knew he needed a believable lie, beyond doubt and beyond questions.

He stood to his feet and crossed the lawn to the guesthouse, his soaked pants clinging to his legs and his white dress shirt carrying stains and tears. He reached the suite and saw Un-hee's suitcase holding open the glass door, still sitting on the threshold where she had abandoned it. Pulling it inside, he closed the door and fell on the bed, staring up at the ceiling. The room continued to sit in darkness, lit only to a dirty yellow through the windows facing the hotel. Ju-han closed his eyes and sensed the rage that had filled his heart earlier was gone; his body was numb and he felt nothing, inside or out. His mind swirled around in a storm of its own, images flashing and vanishing through his head making him unable to focus on anything.

And Un-hee's white form yet floated inside his eyelids.

Still numb, he stood up and walked over to the bathroom. He sparked a hotel match to life and coaxed the flame onto a candle standing beside the sink. Turning on the water, he watched the liquid glass sparkle in the candlelight as it streamed through his hands. He threw some onto his face. Reaching behind, he grasped for a towel, but his hand closed around the hem of Un-hee's silky white hanbok, hanging from the bathroom door. Turning towards it, he stared at the fabric as it shone like a sunlit cloud in his hand.

A plan seeped into his mind.

Pulling it off the hook, he rushed out of the bathroom and tossed the dress onto the bed. Then he skirted around to the other side and retrieved his black tuxedo jacket from where it still lay on the floor. He grabbed the hanbok and dashed out the door into the torrent of water bearing down from the sky.

When he reached the place where Un-hee had leapt to her death, Ju-han hurled the hanbok over the cliff into the ocean. "Here's your precious dress!" he cried, watching it toss in the wind on its way down to the rocks. "You can wear it in death!" Then he removed his jacket and rubbed both sides into the grass, thoroughly soaking it. Finally, he ran back towards the hotel, breaking into wild screams as he neared the lobby.

He pulled open the double doors and stood dead still. The dancing piano music soon ceased, as did the cacophony of many dinner guests' chatter. When all was quiet, every eye in the hall spied Ju-han standing in the doorway; his hair and jacket hanging limp with rain and his bare feet carrying soaked blades of grass. Blood leaked over his nose from three scratches on his forehead where he had gouged himself.

After a moment, a strained wail escaped his teeth, and his stricken stare met the surprise of onlookers as he slowly slipped across the hall to the front desk. The hushed crowd parted before him and hotel staff followed quickly behind, wiping away his drenched, grass-stained footprints.

"She's gone, my bride is gone," Ju-han sobbed to the clerk. "There's no sign of her. I can't find her anywhere."

Behind his glasses, Jung-lee's eyes widened. "Where did you last see her, sir?"

"She said she wanted to go for a walk in the rain with her hanbok on. I told her she shouldn't go outside. She said she wouldn't be gone long. She told me," Ju-han shook his finger in the clerk's face, "she told me she wasn't going to be long!"

Ju-han paused, wiped his face with his sleeve, and sobbed some more. "I went out just a minute after she left to see where she was, and I couldn't find her anywhere. I ran all over the grounds. She's gone." He hung his head over the counter forming beaded pools of water on the wood.

"Sir, perhaps she's just lost out there. It's quite a storm. Try not to worry, just give us a minute and we'll find her." Jung-lee turned to the other clerk standing next to him. "Get us some flashlights, and turn on all the lawn lights. And bring as many employees with you as you can find."

The other clerk rushed away.

"Don't fear, sir. We'll find your lost bride."

Just then, Colonel Cho approached the front desk. He wrapped his arm around Ju-han's shoulders and shook him while his other hand clasped his wine glass. "Well, look who came

99

back for a little nightcap!" Rubbing Ju-han's soaked mess of hair, he added, "You should be more careful, sholdier. You got yourshelf a bit wet there." He swayed forwards and then backwards as he cocked his head and emptied his glass.

"Colonel, I can't stay, I can't talk. There's been a terrible tragedy. I have to go." Ju-han stepped around him to follow the clerk in the search for his bride. The Colonel caught him by the arm.

"Wait jushta shecond there, my eager markshman. What is the nature of the tragic circumshtanshes and how can I be of some ashishtance?" Cho's eyes weren't able to focus on anything anymore, and his sentences were one long word slurred together. "I am ever willing to aid a fellow servisheman in need." The Colonel thumped his chest with his glass.

"Un-hee is gone, Colonel. She went out for a walk in the rain and she has disappeared. I can't find her anywhere." Ju-han tried to free his arm from the Colonel's clutch.

"Well, in that case, I am both your guide and your comfort, my shon. I shaw your bejeweled bride in the wesht hall not three minutes ago."

Ju-han stared at the drunken man in disbelief. "That's impossible. That couldn't have been her."

"As shurely as I thirsht for my next glass, I shaw her there." Cho held Ju-han's arm tightly and thrust an unsteady finger in the direction of the west wing, beyond the rows of tables and hanging chandeliers.

"Show me," the groom replied, and fell in beside the Colonel as the party guests thinned before them, still staring at the sight Ju-han provided for them.

A thorough tour of the torchlit hall produced no sign of Un-hee. The Colonel couldn't understand where she had gone, and was left slurring to himself and searching for a drink while Ju-han hurried outside to join the search party scouring the spacious lawns behind the hotel.

Already they had swept over most of the area, and only the cliff's edge and the adjacent stand of pine trees remained unchecked. The rain fell in thick drops set alight by the powerful beams positioned around the perimeter of the grounds.

"I'm very, very sorry, sir. We haven't been able to find a trace of her yet," Jung-lee exclaimed as he spotted Ju-han running towards the searchers. "You should stay inside until we have some news."

"No, I want to look too. I have to find her." Ju-han's face glistened with water as his eyes settled upon the section of missing rail yawning into darkness under the piercing lights.

"Why is the barrier broken over there?" he asked the clerk as he marched towards it.

"I've never seen it like that before. Maybe you should…" he tried to hold Ju-han from approaching the cliff. Ju-han pushed past him and rushed forward while Jung-lee hurriedly called the other search groups over.

"Bring one of those powerful lights up here," he barked at the worried clerk, who scampered away.

As Ju-han waited by himself at the edge, a surreal encounter occurred. He could see nothing in the darkness below, but the furious waves smashing against the cliff seemed to be calling him, calling his name. He ignored it as hallucination at first and refused to listen, but soon their thunder became unavoidable; they were communicating with him. As he blinked into the weeping wind, he realized the sea was laughing at him, mocking his plight in roaring chorus. The waves knew him, knew who he was, and they also knew that Un-hee had leapt from the cliff to escape from him. They jeered Ju-han and told him they had saved her: the swell had risen and caught her body before she had smashed against the rocks.

Then it ended. The moment was over as quickly as it had begun, and the angry sea below returned to its familiar tune of waves crashing against rocks.

Above, Ju-han sat in stunned silence on the grass, thinking he's slowly lurching towards insanity. But for the first time, the chance that Un-hee had actually survived the fall passed through his head, and he realized if she had, she would have escaped him and death in the same leap. A sickness spread through his chest, and he knew he needed to locate her, whether alive or her lifeless body, to know without doubt.

An instant later, the clerk joined Ju-han at the cliff with a spotlight and together they trained it on the shore and surf below. Soon, all the searchers were huddled about and struggling for a glimpse, at first seeing nothing inside the brilliant circle but a frothing sea churned about by blades of wind, the water crashing like waves of milk onto a shore of coal. As they panned the beam back and forth, it washed over a dazzling shred of cloth lashed to some boulders. The crush of onlookers gasped together with one voice, everyone except Ju-han.

In that instant, he felt cheated that the hanbok had been seen first, and not Un-hee's body. He covered himself by screaming in astonishment and trembling, causing the light to flail about as he shook. Many hands quickly pried him away from the edge.

"My Un-hee, my bride!" he yelled as he collapsed backwards onto the grass and again saw the branches stretching their dark fingers over him.

Jung-lee bent down, his rain-streaked glasses hovering over Ju-han as he tried to calm him. "I am terribly sorry, sir. Please try to stay still. We are calling the authorities –"

Ju-han silenced the clerk by sitting up and grabbing him by the shoulders. His eyes burned wildly. "I must get down there right now. I must be with her. Where is the way down?" He shook the clerk so violently that his glasses slipped off his nose and into his hands.

"There is no way down, sir," Jung-lee stammered as he shoved his spectacles back on his face. "You can't reach that part of the cliff from here."

"There is a way. There must be a way."

"I'm sorry, sir. It's impossible to…"

"Show me!" Ju-han pulled the frightened clerk to within an inch of his face so that their noses were almost touching. His grip tightened Jung-lee's vest around his neck like a vise.

"This way, please, this way, sir. Come with me," the clerk blurted, his fingers pleading with Ju-han's wrists. Ju-han released the trembling man and together they ran along the hedged perimeter of the lawn, the rain slashing against their seaward sides.

Soon, they reached a small break in the bushes near the western wall of the hotel. Here, thick pine trees hid the trail's entrance with spiny arms hanging low about their knees. Jung-lee held the branches aside and together they stepped from the lit perimeter into absolute black. The clerk flicked on his flashlight and the two continued deeper into the trees, following a trail that twisted down the forested slope. Ju-han stubbed his toes several times on the wet stones that marked the path and on the roots that often reached across from both sides to choke it. With each stumble, he released a series of curses and finally demanded that he hold the flashlight. Far above, the wind lashed at the peaks of the trees but was not able to cut through the forest with any strength. Amid the creaking and groaning of the pines, Ju-han prodded the clerk to maintain pace.

When they had reached the edge of the forest, Ju-han again felt the full wrath of the storm. Wind-driven sheets of rain stung his face and neck, and forced his eyes closed if he looked towards the ocean. The path flattened and they crossed a small bridge arching its back over a gurgling stream.

"I'll need the flashlight again, sir," cried Jung-lee above the gale once they had gained the bridge. "I will show you where we need to go."

Ju-han handed the torch back and the clerk trained the yellow beam on some stone stairs to the left that fell away steeply into darkness. Wind from the ocean tore up the staircase and tried to shred the men's clothes from their limbs. Cautiously, they began stepping down the rock-hewn steps, walls of black lava growing on both sides until they were engulfed in the stone reaching above their heads. Ju-han felt along the wet rock with his hands and slowly followed Jung-lee, not trusting his bare feet on the slimy stairs.

The steep channel bent to the left and suddenly the roar of plunging water burst out upon them. The wall of rock behind Ju-han's left hand fell away and he staggered forward as the growling cascade rung in his ears. Luckily, he was able to steady himself on the clerk's shoulder and together, they continued descending the stairs. The chorus of falling water on their left began to mingle with the rolling thunder of waves in front of them.

When they had reached the last stair, Jung-lee turned about with his golden torch and lit the waterfall behind them as it spewed out from under the forest's fringe. The freshwater crashed into a pool that was overfull and rippled over dark stones into the salty surf pounding in to meet it. A rope railing swayed between cement stumps, fencing the men from the angry ocean.

"This is as far as we can go," Jung-lee shouted into Ju-han's ear. The wind swept off the sea and clawed at both of them.

"Where is Un-hee?" cried Ju-han.

"The place she fell from is around the corner of that cliff."

Ju-han looked across the small bay that frothed at his feet and saw the clerk's beam paint a weak circle on a wall of rock. "The only way to get over there and around to the other side is by boat," Jung-lee shouted. And then he quickly added, "But the hotel doesn't have one."

"My bride! Un-hee!" Ju-han yelled into the mouth of the storm. He stood with the clerk on a dais of stone that had been washed with centuries of rain. The worn rock had endured the punishment of being placed between a tireless waterfall ever spilling beside it and ceaseless waves forever pounding against it.

As Ju-han stood pinched between these two powers, he clenched the rope railing in futile hands and felt complete helplessness for the first time in his life. Never had he experienced such a total loss of control, and the burning plate of anger surged within him again. Un-hee had escaped him, and though she might have paid for it with her life, he felt only betrayal. He stood on the platform and refused to cry, though a sea of salty tears pounded before his eyes.

eight

The water felt warm and violent. But she speared through the churning surface of the sea into its still depths, and suddenly, in an instant, all was muted and darkly subtle as though time and space had divided around her. Gone were the lightning and tearing wind; the stinging rain had vanished, even the terror of falling no longer shook her. All that remained was warm darkness in every direction.

I must be dead, she thought. I'm floating in the world of dreams and spirits, suspended in a black void and surrounded by nothing.

Though at first she was wrapped in numbness, a burning sensation soon grew in her chest. As the heat spread, flashes within her brain brought vanishing slides to her eyes: still frames of dark trees backlit by terrific slashes of lightning, and Ju-han's face snarling with bared fangs like a hunted animal. Though she tried to avoid seeing the slides, wherever she turned, there they were: flashes of the hotel and hall, the fountain surrounded by partying guests, the buffet tables overflowing with food, and Colonel Cho draining another glass of wine while his eyes swam around in his head. The bursting images scrolled and evaporated repeatedly in front of her, faster and faster, as the flames within her lungs continued to grow.

Suddenly, everything vanished, leaving behind red letters that burned before her in the darkness and stung her eyes.

I jumped for freedom, though I bore no chains,
He killed his bride, though he bears no stain.

The words melted together and formed a blaze that roared through her chest. The fire reached up her throat and licked at her tongue, and she realized she needed breath. Stricken by a sudden panic, she began clawing at the inky night surrounding her, desperately fighting for the surface.

Un-hee burst into the heart of the storm drinking in delicious oxygen. Her white-hot lungs immediately began to cool. She had broken the surface some distance from shore where the tide's rip had pulled her, and the surrounding ocean was a swirling cauldron of fury as rolling walls of water swept over her, making the struggle for air equally as desperate on the surface. Her pajamas, though light, glued her every movement to the surging sea and made staying afloat even more difficult. Lightning continued to ignite the darkness sporadically, and its cracking tail of thunder joined with the ocean's roar to shatter down around Un-hee and disorient her further. She could see nothing when the piercing white wands extinguished; every direction was deepest night. And she could never anticipate the waves that continually punished her into submission below the surface. They were fast soaking up her remaining strength, and in her fight for air, she took in several mouthfuls of saltwater, making her nauseous. She had yet to recover her breath from the initial plunge and every assaulting wall of water further leaked her energy and will.

One double shard of lightning made every surrounding drop of rain blaze as a fallen diamond. Beyond their brilliance, Un-hee glimpsed the dark face of the cliff frowning down upon her. In a weary daze, she realized she must be nearing shore; the waves were pushing her in. As the light vanished and thunder growled from the throat of the storm, Un-hee felt a powerful wave pull her into its rolling teeth. She tried to swim in front of it but managed only to swallow more seawater as the wave flipped her several times and threw her violently onto the boulders guarding the coastline. The wave retreated leaving Un-hee draped like a wet rag over a sea-smoothed stone.

She struggled to move, knowing that another torturous wave would descend at any moment, but she couldn't. Her left arm was folded in pain and lay hidden beneath her. She braced her feet against a rock behind her and pushed with both legs off the stone. Falling to the pebbly ground, she sat up and hid behind the rock as another wave's roar grew behind her. Tumbling thunder filled the air as water and foam lashed the shore all about Un-hee, nearly wrenching her from her hiding place. As the wave pulled back out to sea, it wrapped her against the stone with its binding current.

After the water subsided, she struggled to her feet and stumbled as fast as she could towards higher ground, fleeing the ocean's tortured edges. She managed to climb fast enough and the next wave could only lick her heels as she reached the cliff's roots. Rain continued to whip against her weakened frame while the wind seemed more furious than ever here at the wall of rock, protesting the resistance by tearing up its face.

Un-hee slumped over and leaned against the stone wall with her shoulder. Her pajamas hung as dripping rags of cloth and her left arm throbbed in pain. Her head ached from being starved of air, and she squeezed her temples together to keep her skull from splitting in two. All around her, she felt the storm's claws, but she could no longer hear its violence: she saw only Ju-han's snarling teeth and heard only his biting words. She wished him dead, wished she could have been more powerful than him; but instead, she had to flee into the night from the one who had murdered her inside. He was still alive somewhere far above while under that cliff, death filled her lungs and decay seeped from her nostrils. She hadn't tried to commit suicide; she was already a corpse even as she fell.

Yet her shell lived on. She wondered if he would search for her, and whether he believed she was dead. She knew she should be, and though she couldn't fully appreciate the miracle at present, she was grateful to have escaped Ju-han with her life. There, between a wall of lava and an ocean of hate, she resolved never to let him see her again.

After her heaving breaths subsided and air filled her lungs once again, she lifted her head and defied the storm; the lightning, searing from the soaked clouds, lit her eyes with dark fire and resolve. She knew she would have to move quickly to evade Ju-han, for there would be a search. Stumbling along the shore, she skimmed her right hand against the jagged stone wall while her left arm hung useless before the sea. Her bare feet bled between the rocks, blades of frozen lava slicing her skin, while the surf continued to pound next to her and sometimes reached up her battered legs with larger swells.

Painfully, she progressed along the beach until she rounded the face of the cliff, now enduring the storm's onslaught on her back, and only as a glancing blow because of the stone shield beside her. Cascading thunder shook the closed bay she faced, where the waterfall whispered in its deepest corner. Frequent shards of lightning washed the entire shoreline in platinum as Un-hee sought any shelter she could find nearby to conceal her bruised frame. Her body needed a respite soon or she would collapse where she stood.

One such illumination showed her a glimpse of a tunnel winking from the far side of the bay near the waterfall. Un-hee saw it's dark eye peeled within a ghostly second of brilliance, and vanish when night's coat wrapped about again with choking speed. She decided that if it were a cave, it would offer her the best secret refuge available.

While she pressed on, she found her mind running to Ju-han, even as her body still fought to flee him. But return she did, in thought, though out of fear, to the man of her ruin. She remembered his obsessiveness, his thirst for control, and the more she contemplated his mind, she understood he would not rest until he found her. And if she were not dead when he did, he would ensure the remainder of her life with him would be a living death.

The black rocks under Un-hee's feet gradually sloped downwards as the dark waters crested higher next to her. Soon the waves sealed off the shoreline in front of her and pressed against the cliff wall to trap her progress. Her toes waded into the water and she saw that she could walk no farther. To reach the far side of the small cove, she had only one option: she would have to swim across.

Though her left forearm protested each movement with spiking pain in all directions and her feet wept bloody tears with every step, her will determined her course. Her iron resolve sprung from the cracks in her heart of stone, and had long burrowed in ground ripe for unforgiveness. The weightiest decisions of her life leading up this night had been made for her by men who knew little or nothing about her. Each one had left a stone within her until they blocked all hurt and all joy from ever entering, and since Shin-char's death, she had taught herself to feel nothing.

But as Un-hee leapt from the cliff, she fell free because her load of rocks had not followed her. For the first time in her life, she had taken a step of her own and that single leap had torn the power of futility, which had bound her in stone chains. The decision had been hers, and the consequences she owned. However, she understood her dire situation: even if she was able to escape, an arduous journey still lay before her on the other side. But beyond all, she would be free to choose each step.

She passed between two boulders and waded back into the dark waves. Her feet welcomed the wet warmth on their soles. At that moment, had she scanned the upper reaches of the cliff with the help of a lightning strike, she would have noticed an oddity jutting out of the stone face above: a single tooth of rock, crowned with leaves and clinging near the top.

She eased ahead until the water circled her waist, and then she kicked off the rock bottom and floated forward. The waves pounded less here since they arrived tattered and broken from the cliff's foremost nose of stone. A wave swept Un-hee from the shore, and she swam only enough to stay afloat because of the stabbing pain in her arm. To her surprise, the waves bore her as though they knew her mind. When one swell left her and continued to shore, another would gather her to its crest and carry her farther.

Using only her right arm she swam lightly, though she could have managed no greater effort had she tried, and she used her legs when her tired arm cried for rest. Shock had begun to blanket her soaked skin and cracked bones, and fear darkened her mind with thoughts of the pounding shore drawing ever nearer. Un-hee faltered as an anxious cloud fogged her brain, and doubt seeped over her heart like a shadow, whispering failure. Even if she did make it to the far side, she would be slammed against the shore's teeth again, risking death a second time. The rain, driving as snow in the lightning's glory, mesmerized her and stung her brain with pricks of white long after night's curtain had fallen again. She kicked her legs with little force and she could no longer lift her good arm out of the water between strokes. Her strength drained and she floated where the black sea moved her, without rudder and without power.

When she thought she could stay afloat no longer, Un-hee slipped deeper into the sea. But instead of drowning, her feet touched smooth pebbles and she was able to stand on them; they felt hard and cool and strong beneath her toes. She waded slowly towards shore and again heard the rush of heavy water, but only gentle foaming rollers wrapped about her waist. The pounding seemed to fall down to her from somewhere high above, ahead of her.

She emerged from the ocean a dripping frame, still being supported by the wind-driven waves. As she reached safer ground, she was surprised to hear the growling surf behind her again, and when the clouds stabbed their white swords down from the sky, Un-hee saw the crushing waves had returned and were again punishing the rocks along the shore that held them back.

Still the rhythmic churning sang in her ears. With more lightning flashing, she turned and saw a silver waterfall pouring from black stone; its tongue of platinum fell to spreading mists that shrouded the sea foam sliding up to its feet. Suddenly, as she looked higher, she saw a blade of light swinging side to side as it descended through a narrow channel of rock beside the waterfall.

Terror clenched Un-hee's heart and she started scrambling up the rocky shore as fast as she could. She needed to get away from the naked beach, and hide under the cover of the cliff before she was spotted. She saw the liquid swathe of gold slide lower and lower as she forced her legs to pump faster, shredding her soles ever more. She reached the wall of stone and crouched beside it, her back heaving with breath. She hoped against fear whoever held the light wouldn't scan the shore with it.

A few moments later, she saw a bleak sun roaming along the face of the far cliff, the very wall she had been unable to follow earlier. She dropped her head on her knees and wished with all her soul that it wouldn't swing around in her direction, for she had nowhere to run.

She heard the faint sound of a man's voice tossing in the storm as it argued with another. Un-hee could catch only snatches of the heated voice while the replies were utterly stripped by the wind before they ever reached her. Then she heard a rending scream that froze her skin.

"My bride! Un-hee!"

The cry tore from Ju-han's throat and wrapped around Un-hee like cords of steel. He had seen her. He was running up the stony beach. He would soon seize her in fists of iron clenched tighter than ever before, and would drag her back into his world of abuse and power. What cursed fate could have led him to her after she had nearly died escaping his hold on the other side of the bluffs? She pressed her head against her knees and waited for his punishing grip.

It never came.

When she finally looked up, the yellow beam was gone, the waterfall yet spilled nearby, and the waves pounded even harder before her salty eyes. She was still free. She breathed relief and thanked the night for wrapping her in its blanket. Standing stiffly, Un-hee started wandering along the shore away from hotel and waterfall, hoping to find the cave entrance before she collapsed for good.

Creeping slowly along the beach, she leaned on the cliff for support while the waves reached up foaming lips to kiss the wind as it cried over them. By the time it reached the shore, the wind's fury would not be resisted and it ravaged the offending coastline that dared stand so tall in defiance. One such violent assault threw Un-hee towards the cliff but instead of support, her right hand fell into nothing. She stumbled to the ground and knew she lay at the threshold of the cave. Crawling into the tunnel in the rock, she stood carefully and protected her head from the unseen ceiling. She found the rock above stooped just low enough to prevent her from walking upright. Bending her head, Un-hee began to probe deeper into the cave, wanting to distance herself from the rain and raging wind. She was thankful for the stillness and dryness of the burrow, and the smooth stone felt like velvet under her battered feet.

But inside the tunnel was absolute pitch; Un-hee couldn't see her hand though she held it to her nose. Even the flashes from the storm behind her could lay only a weak luster at the doorstep. She shuffled forward in the darkness, holding her right arm outstretched into the ink in front of her while her left hand rubbed lightly against the wall.

After some halting progress, her foot stubbed against a stone sitting in the middle of the cave. She decided she could go no further, and laid her exhausted body on the floor and placed the rock under her head. The storm's fury was but a distant howl here, where lightning filled the cave's oval eye with a shield of white, and thunder rumbled in and crawled past her ears to die somewhere beneath the island.

Un-hee didn't stir once, and soon fell into a heavy sleep. The rock became her bed and the stone above her covers, and they afforded her better rest in the shape of a cave than she could ever hope to achieve lying next to the man that had been her husband. Her bones ached, her arm throbbed and her feet bled, but she knew none of it while she slept. She was only happy to be free.

And free she remained while asleep, liberated from all woe and hurt, until her dreams began. Though her body cried for rest, her fatigued mind continued to labour in the darkness, bringing her other, more serious cares.

She was trapped in a tunnel. At one end, waves taller than trees surged towards her while at the other, a giant tiger with red eyes stood on his hind legs and advanced with claws splayed open. Both threats meant certain death, and they approached Un-hee with equal speed, neither closing in faster than the other. Un-hee looked from one end to the other and saw no escape, and though the waves shook the cave with terrible power, she feared the tiger more.

As she watched the great cat pounding closer, his face melted before her eyes: his fur dissolved into skin and thinned into human hair on top of his head, his nose shrunk and blanched until a person's nostrils formed, and his ears descended, their edges thawing and reshaping into a man's ears. Un-hee continued to stare in fear as the tiger's eyes narrowed and lowered until she was looking into human pupils that burned crimson from a human skull. Only the fangs changed not, and continued gnashing behind curled lips.

Un-hee suddenly recognized whose head the tiger wore: Ju-han's!

She touched both slimy walls as she faced the snarling menace. Though the cave was small, the tiger dwarfed her looking down through hot coals blazing from his eye sockets. She backed away slowly and then started running in the opposite direction. The waves loomed high above her and plunged down in a rush of white. She could see flashes of lightning through the wall of water, and as she screamed into the fury of the wave, her cry was swallowed by its torrent. The surge was about to bury her when suddenly the tiger slashed her left side from behind with his claw, and she fell to the stone floor with her forearm broken underneath her. Pain seared through her arm and body as she screamed again into the wet rock.

nine

By the time Ju-han and the clerk stepped back into the bright perimeter of the hotel, policemen and soldiers were milling over the entire rear lawn. The grounds resembled a battlefield. Two rifle-bearing sentinels immediately approached the men and demanded their names and identification. Jung-lee showed them his name tag and continued to fumble through his vest for his hotel employee card, but at the mention of Ju-han's name, both of them were piloted directly towards the cliff edge and the broken railing.

As he marched into the soaking wind, Ju-han looked around with apprehension at the sudden and heavy presence of the military. He wished Colonel Cho were outside with him, and sober, so he could have some martial weight on his side. Between gusts as he peered ahead, he could see a tight knot of black hooded jackets bowing under the pine trees. The flaring hate within him had cooled on the way up from the ocean to settle as an uneasy load on the floor of his chest. The more Ju-han watched the surrounding soldiers, the heavier the burden inside grew so that, by the time the guards had ushered them to the dark circle of rifles and raincoats, he carried an anvil within his plastic ribcage.

The crowd opened and spread into a semi-circle in front of Ju-han and the clerk. The escorting soldiers were waved off and a short officer in the center of the group stepped forward.

"Good evening, gentlemen," his voice rasped from a throat full of wet gravel. "I am General Jin. I believe we're interested in hearing from you." His thin nose and pocked cheeks shone in the hotel's golden light, but the wide brim of his hood wrapped his eyes in shadow.

"Good evening, General," Jung-lee erupted. "I am head clerk at the front desk of the Sunrise and I'm so glad you're here." His voice quivered with emotion. "Have you been told everything yet?"

"Yes, thank you. Your colleagues were able to provide most of the facts, but my men would like to go over some finer points with you right now, if that's possible," Jin answered, waving his arm towards the other officers.

"Of course, right away," jumped the clerk. The black hoods swallowed him into their midst and they all trudged off towards the hotel, leaving Ju-han and the General standing alone at the cliff edge.

"And I would like to go through everything with you, Mr. Kim, as soon as possible," rasped the General.

"Couldn't this all wait until tomorrow?" asked Ju-han as he wiped rain from his face. "I've had a very difficult night and I'm badly in need of rest."

"Sorry, Mr. Kim, it can't," the General scratched in reply. "The information is fresh in your mind right now, and we need all available details to find out exactly what happened to your wife."

"Won't you guys be busy getting her body tonight?" Ju-han twisted again as he tried to peak into the darkness cloaking the General's eyes. The anchor within his chest continued to weigh him down, and this military man's persistence caused it to mire ever deeper.

General Jin stood unmoved for several seconds before he shook his head a little. "That's impossible while this storm lasts, Mr. Kim," he scraped. "We could never get a boat near that shore without breaking up on the rocks. We will go when it's light, the storm won't stay much past morning."

"Tomorrow morning? You mean you're just going to leave her down there to be smashed against the rocks all night? I can't accept that, sir. I won't accept it." Ju-han's breath heaved from his mouth. "No, General. I want her body retrieved right now." He pointed a dripping finger in the General's face.

"Mr. Kim, I know it's hard for you to understand given your situation, but I assure you, that's completely impossible. Everything will be taken care of once the sun comes up and the storm lifts."

Ju-han looked over at the mass of soldiers scouring the hedges and perimeter of the hotel. "I curse this storm and all that it has brought."

General Jin pulled on Ju-han's arm and the two started crossing the lawn towards the hotel. "We'll use your suite for the questioning," Jin rasped as they neared the guesthouse sitting dark and still beneath the hotel's glowing face.

Ju-han stopped while his mind raced for an excuse. "We can't. It's… It hasn't had power all night," he protested.

The General's lips parted in a slow smirk. "The power has returned while you were away. Let me show you." He placed his hand on Ju-han's shoulder and pressed him forward.

They slipped across the drenched lawn in silence until they reached the glass doors of the honeymoon suite. The General opened the door and held it while Ju-han led the way inside. He flicked on the light switch just inside the door and, as the room filled with light, quickly spun around to see the General's reaction, a smug grin of confidence. Ju-han looked into his eyes for the first time as Jin held his gaze for a moment. The General's eyebrows formed tangled strips of grey moss above his eyes, two shining black stones floating on snow. They were set close together as though they were magnets pulling at each other under the bony bridge of his nose.

The moment broke and General Jin peeled off his long raincoat revealing a stiffly pressed military uniform underneath, sparkling with war medals. When he removed his cap, his black hair bowed short and stiff upon his head. In the light, his face was even more pocked than Ju-han had seen earlier, and a scarlet stripe sliced over his right cheekbone. They sat down together at the table near the window.

"I understand your grief, and I apologize for having to do this immediately," Jin began, producing a pad and pen from inside his jacket.

Ju-han nodded silently as he swept soaked hair away from his eyes.

"And so I will be brief," the General continued. "How long have you known your wife?"

"Almost three months."

"When did you last see her?"

"She was excited about the storm and wanted to go out to see what it was like, to feel the rain and the wind. So she ran out the door and said she would be right back." Ju-han leaned his forehead on the heel of his hand. "That's the last time I saw her."

"Thank you, but can you tell me what time that was, sir?"

"Oh, I can't say for sure, maybe around 11:00 at night."

"What did you do then?" The General wrote the entire time, not bothering to look up even to ask the questions. When he talked, his voice sounded like sandpaper rubbing against stone in Ju-han's ears. Ju-han tried to peek at the writing on the pad but Jin's cap sat on the table directly in front of him, blocking the view.

"Well, she was wearing her wedding hanbok and everything so I didn't think she'd be gone very long. But she didn't return after about a minute or two so I went outside and looked around for her."

"And what did you find?"

"Well, I didn't find anything. She had completely disappeared. I searched all over the entire lawn area here, and even up in the bushes along the side of the hotel, yelling and calling for her." Ju-han covered his face and coughed. "Finally, I went into the hotel and told the head clerk that my wife is outside somewhere and she's missing."

The General kept scratching in his pad. "And what happened then?"

"We went outside with many of the hotel staff and spread out. At first, we found nothing. But after some searching, we found the railing was missing in one spot near the cliff. We used one of the lights to look over the edge and we saw her hanbok on the rocks far below."

"Did you see her body?"

"No, probably because the storm was too fierce to be able to see that clearly."

"What did you do then?"

"Well, I wanted the hotel staff to go and get her from those awful rocks and waves but they kept insisting there was no way to get to her without a boat. So I had the clerk lead me down to the water to see if this was true. That's where we were returning from when we found you guys all over the place up here."

The General nodded and continued writing furiously on the paper. "And when you went down to the ocean, is that where you got those cuts in your forehead?" He pointed at Ju-han's head with the end of his pen.

"Umm... no," Ju-han answered, rubbing the scars as he hesitated. "When I went searching in the bushes next to the hotel on the far side, some branches scratched my face."

"Which side was that exactly?"

Timo Annala

"I guess that would have been… that side," Ju-han answered, pointing vaguely over his left shoulder.

"I see." Jin paused and wrote some more. "And when you were searching around by yourself, before you had gone into the hotel, did you see the break in the railing then?"

"No, I didn't."

The General looked up, perching a bushy eyebrow. "Why not?"

"It was too dark to see anything. You should see this back lawn area when they have all the perimeter lights shut off. The place is blacker than night."

"I see," Jin replied, dropping his eyes to the pad. "Is there any chance you know an army colonel by the name Cho?"

"I do. Why?"

"He might have mentioned seeing you in the hotel lobby when you were searching for your wife." The General looked up again from his writing.

"Yes, that's right. I did talk to him briefly when I went in to see the clerk."

"Why didn't you mention that earlier?"

"I didn't think it was important. Is it?"

"That depends, sir. What was said?"

"Oh, nothing that makes any sense. The Colonel was beyond drunk and could hardly stand on his own. He mumbled something about seeing my wife in the hotel shortly before I came in looking for her. I told him to show me where she was so we took a walk through the banquet hall but couldn't find her." Ju-han rested his head in his hands again. "And now I know why."

General Jin wrote in silence for a while and then looked up at Ju-han. "Mr. Kim, was your wife glad to marry you?"

Ju-han glanced up quickly. "Of course she was. She was in love with me, and we were on our honeymoon at a fabulous hotel. Why do you ask?"

Jin ignored the question. "Was there anything in her behaviour today or tonight that seemed odd? Was she, perhaps, moody, agitated or sad about anything?"

"No, not at all. We were very happy and very excited to be married. What are you getting at? Do you think she wanted to die? You think she killed herself?"

"I don't think anything right now, Mr. Kim. I'm merely being thorough."

"Well, that's one possibility you can rule out right away, General. She was extremely happy to be married to me. Ask anyone at the hotel, she hardly left my side all night."

The General chewed on the end of his pen. "Where is your home, Mr. Kim?"

"I live in Gwanju City. Why?"

"We may need to contact you for more information as our investigation progresses. Please, don't leave the hotel without seeing me."

"How long will all this take?"

"No more than a few days."

"When will you be able to rescue her from the water?" Ju-han sighed, suddenly feeling limp and tired.

"We should be able to reach her shortly after dawn."

"Can you let me know as soon as you've brought her out?"

"We will."

Ju-han stood and rubbed his eyes with the heels of his hands. "Well, if that's everything, I'd like to get some rest."

"Just about," the General answered, standing and adjusting his jacket. "I only have one more question regarding your honeymoon suite: why were there wet footprints in here as we entered? Didn't you say you went immediately to the front desk when you couldn't find your wife outside?" He looked up at Ju-han as he finished the question.

"What is this? Are you saying I'm not telling you the truth?"

"Not at all," Jin replied, his voice rasping a level monotone. "I'm only trying to put all the pieces together to find out how this all happened."

"Those tracks were probably from the guys that fixed the lights in here. Someone had to get them to work again."

"Oh yes, you're probably right. That must have been what happened." General Jin threw his raincoat back on and tucked his dark hair beneath his cap. "I can see why they would need to go into the bathroom to repair the power," he added, pulling open the door.

He turned back and looked into Ju-han's eyes with an unwavering stare. "Thank you for your cooperation, Mr. Kim. We'll be in touch." Bowing slightly, he turned and ducked out of the door, back into the wind and rain.

Ju-han's cheeks burned as the gale pushed the glass door closed with a thud. He clenched his fists and cursed the General for being so suspicious of him, especially without evidence. Ju-han returned to the table and stared through the window at the herd of soldiers and police milling around the spot where Un-hee had leapt to her death.

I didn't do anything wrong, he mused, watching the bitter fruit this night had bore. I was her husband, and she was my bride. She owed herself to me, and she brought only pain on herself by resisting. Had she given in, had she just yielded, everything would have been right. If only Un-hee had submitted, he wished, hating the word. Instead, he had married a selfish woman who had refused him. Her defiance, he reasoned, had corroded her thoughts and turned to insanity in her mind. He was certain madness had finally pushed her over that cliff. She was confused and delusional, and didn't see that he was trying to help her, not hurt her.

Ju-han watched the army patrols pass back and forth in front of the lights, and a sense of betrayal filled his stomach. I showed her the better way; I showed her the proper way, and I've been left to struggle on alone, bearing the chains her defiance fashioned.

He slipped into bed and spread the covers over him, though the warm night wrapped about like a humid blanket. He noticed that Un-hee's fluttering white shape hadn't plagued him since he was down at the ocean, and he was happy to have rid the apparition from his mind. He curled on his side and closed his eyes, striving for the peace of sleep, but the unquiet in his heart refused to be comforted. His head swam on the pillow, and the bursts of lightning flashing in the windows startled him whenever slumber drew near. When Ju-han opened his eyes, the dark shapes and shadows of the room seemed to spin around him in a ghostly procession, and would lure closer if his eyes narrowed. He fought them back by turning on the end table lamp, but still he found no calm; the light had chased away the spirits but also kept him from finding sleep. He tossed back and forth and wearied himself far into the night.

When slumber finally caught him, Ju-han's last conscious thought laid a mantle of anxiety over his dreams: his mind replayed Un-hee's words about her mom and the murderous, traitorous man she had described as his father.

ten

Un-hee was still screaming when she awoke. She was lying face down on her left side, her damaged arm folded beneath her on the rock floor. She winced from the pain as she sat up slowly and leaned against the moist cave wall. Her heart continued to gallop from the tiger but she was relieved to know it had only been a dream and it was over now. She rubbed her eyes and looked towards the cave entrance. The storm had passed taking its dark cloak with it, and the oval doorway beyond winked with pale grey light that blended through the blue mist hanging over the ocean.

Un-hee shivered as she stood up, her wet pajamas still clinging to her skin. Though the air was warm, the moist fabric soaked up every ember of heat in her body and left her chilled. She stumbled painfully towards the cave entrance as her cut feet cried out at every step; the scabs that had just begun to form while she slept were once again ripped open on the hard ground.

As she neared the threshold, she wondered where she could possibly go from here. She had no clothes, no money, and no food, her arm hung broken at her side, and her feet, without bandages and shoes, would not last long on rocky beaches and hard roads. Un-hee's heart quickened inside her and a flutter of doubt again passed a dark wing over her mind. She needed an angel.

She peeked out from the cave at the grey world stretched before her. Tiger Island's sheer walls slept on the calm sea, shrouded in a veil of mist. The sun had not yet lifted the lid of its burning eye over the water, and the coastline around Un-hee still slumbered beneath ghostly shapes of fog. On her left, the waterfall pounded a muted rhythm from behind the stone stairs, and the waves near her feet gently embraced the beach, having no memory of their former violence, not six hours old.

As she stepped out of the rock, a butterfly flew over her shoulder from inside the cave behind her, and circled her head three times, leaping through the air on wings of scarlet edged in gold leaf. Dancing and spinning before her eyes, it moved as a masterpiece of liquid colour, floating on a canvas of cloud.

"Well hello, Goldie," Un-hee greeted the creature as she stared in awe at its brilliance. She reached out her hand and the butterfly alighted as a falling feather on her index finger. It flexed its wings slowly and turned to face the opposite direction, away from the waterfall. When it had finished turning, it again took flight and bobbed in front of her.

"You are definitely the most beautiful butterfly I've ever seen," she remarked. She couldn't even remember spotting this variety before. "I wonder who painted your wings such lovely colours?"

The butterfly continued to flit excitedly through the air, jumping ahead and swirling higher, then returning to Un-hee. Curiosity enveloped her.

"I have never seen any creature behave like you, Goldie. You seem very excited. Are you trying to tell me something?"

Goldie's shining wings fluttered closer to Un-hee and rested on her shoulder. Then the butterfly took to the air again and flew over the rocks for some distance before returning. Un-hee realized it was beckoning her to follow. She took a trial step and the butterfly flew away from her and then returned, as if to find out why Un-hee had stopped. When she stepped again, Goldie flew ahead a second time in expectation.

"All right, Goldie, you have my attention now," she spoke softly to the butterfly. "I have no idea where you want me to go, but I'm glad you're at least leading me away from the hotel."

She hobbled behind the flittering creature, slicing new cuts into her feet with every step over the sharp stones. The light was yet too pale to penetrate the mist, and Un-hee couldn't see into the crevices between the boulders. She limped slowly along the stony beach, leaning on the larger rocks for support and pressing against the cliff wall where necessary. The lava had frozen into jagged shapes when it had met the ocean, and on these serrated teeth Un-hee was forced to march.

She watched the butterfly twisting and skipping in the air ahead of her. "Oh, Goldie! If only I could leap through the air like you can. You have no idea what it's like to be bound to earth, do you?"

She stopped and sat on a boulder to rest her tortured soles. The painted wings returned to her and continued to circle around until she stood up again. "Ok, Goldie, I'll keep coming. But I want you to know that you're not making my feet feel any better. I'm not sure how much more I can manage. It would be nice if I could just climb on your back and you could fly me away to wherever you're taking me."

The duo progressed at a snail's pace down the stone beach, past huge boulders, and rocks pressed into hexagons from the immense heat and elements that were present when the island formed. The mist remained and shrouded the coast with a grey blanket, preventing Un-hee from seeing into the distance. The cliff beside her seemed to be bending further right, and from somewhere ahead, she heard the growl of engines and the shouts of fishermen calling to each other in the morning fog.

Another edge cut into her foot and she could walk no more. The butterfly had led Un-hee an agonizing distance from the cave, and now she had to stop where she stood. She sat on the rounded boulder next to her and dangled her torn feet in the air, flesh hanging from the soles while the loss of blood was sending her legs and body into shock.

"I'm sorry, Goldie," she wept as the butterfly flew back to her and bobbed around her head. "I can't take another step. I guess this is where it ends. Someone will come and find me here, and take me back to that hateful hotel, and to him. Thank you for being my friend for a little while, Goldie. You're too beautiful for this world."

As Un-hee finished speaking, the butterfly spun away from her and twisted higher and higher until it vanished above the green fringe of the cliff. Un-hee watched it fly away, and expected its return at any moment. When it stayed hidden, a pang of sadness stung her heart.

"I'm sorry, Goldie," she whispered to herself. "I didn't mean for you to leave me here. I didn't mean for you to go."

She dropped her gaze and surveyed her surroundings. The lead sea and steel air still mixed together and shaped an impenetrable mist around her. The rocky shoreline stretched away in both directions, but at least she had distanced herself from the hotel, she thought.

Then she stiffened when she heard a noise. Voices... women's voices were drifting from the greyness ahead. They grew stronger and clearer, their laughter and conversation flowing to Un-hee like water rippling over stones. Soon, the first figures began to emerge ghost-like out of the cloud until she saw seven women walking towards her along the beach near the water's edge. They wore black rubber suits from their necks to their ankles, and they carried nets attached to Styrofoam floats while white caps clung to their heads under black diving goggles. Un-hee recognized them as the renowned Jeju diving women.

"Good morning," she called to them. When they had stopped and looked over at her, she beckoned for them to approach.

As they picked their way over the rocky beach, their legs remained bowed and backs hunched from years of heavy labour. Their bodies were resilient and their faces lined and hard. They had weathered many stormy days in pursuing their catch, and the sea and salt were engraved in their skin. Soon, they surrounded Un-hee and stared at her as though she had risen from the tide.

"Good morning, child. What has happened to you?" began the most elderly of the group, standing directly in front of her. Her creased face resembled worn leather and the skin on her neck hung with age, but her eyes winked stamina and wisdom from inside their black pupils.

"It's a long story, sisters," Un-hee spoke to all of them. "One that will leave me closer to death in the telling. I am very badly hurt and would appreciate any help you could give me." She bowed as respectfully as she could while sitting on the boulder.

The diving women saw Un-hee's swollen arm and bleeding feet, and knew her ragged clothes carried evidence of more trauma. The woman spoke again. "We will help you, child. Have no fear. Sisters, let's gather some clothes and food for this desperate soul."

As the women sifted through their bags, the senior diver approached Un-hee with some bandages. "My poor child, let me wrap you up, your feet look horrible. My name is Lee Soo-mee. Don't worry, we will help you with whatever you need."

Her eyes settled gently on Un-hee's fragile face. They were clearer than Un-hee had seen earlier, and as dark as coal, but they carried a soft light that made Un-hee feel safe.

With strong hands, Soo-mee held Un-hee's feet steady as she wrapped them in clean cloth. Un-hee watched as the woman worked with care and skill, but also with speed belying her age. Every movement was efficiency itself. Un-hee stared at Soo-mee's fingers and was amazed: they were hard and knotted, bronzed by the elements, and could no longer be straightened after decades of toil in the sea. And yet, in their strength was gentleness, and they wrapped around her feet with a supple touch. To Un-hee, they more resembled tools than hands at the ends of her arms.

Once her feet were bandaged, Un-hee watched another diving woman approach and set a pair of leather-soled slippers over the dressings, while a third woman worked a coarse, brown shirt and matching pants onto her body. Soon, they had her surrounded again and fashioned a cloth sling for her arm, which Soo-mee snuck beneath her shirt. Through their tenderness, Un-hee felt whole again, as though her naked and wounded body and heart had been clothed with love.

When they had finished their duties, six of the diving women gathered up their baskets and, nodding farewell to Un-hee and Soo-mee on the shore, waded back into the ocean. They slipped their goggles over their eyes and were soon diving below the surface and filling their baskets with food from the sea.

"Come sit over here on this flat stone, child," Soo-mee directed. She began digging through the basket beside her. "You must be starving."

"Actually, yes, sister, I am," Un-hee admitted, settling on the rock beside the elderly woman.

Soo-mee retrieved some muscles and clams from the basket. "Here is the freshest, healthiest breakfast you can have to feed some life back into your poor soul," she announced, shaking the excess water from them. "We just pulled them from the ebbing tide this morning."

Un-hee again watched in fascination as Soo-mee's gnarled hands dug inside the shells and scooped out the meat with her little finger shaped like a hook of iron. Her forehead bore rippled skin that carried the cares of many years in its creases. Un-hee wondered how old she was, and how long she had been a diving woman. She had undoubtedly seen the terrible effects of wars and occupation for she had lived through times of great unrest for Korea. Un-hee wanted to ask her questions and find answers to her own. She saw a lot of her grandmother in Soo-mee's lined face, and she longed for her strength and love.

"Eat up, child," Soo-mee commanded, passing Un-hee a metal platter filled with several different piles of seafood, as well as side dishes of garlic, kimchi, and a paste made of red peppers, dried and crushed.

Un-hee dove in at once and savoured the tastes of the sea. Her stomach had twisted into a knot through the night, and only slowly did it unravel as she sent food down to it. Soo-mee laughed seeing her gulp the food, and Un-hee chuckled with her, watching the elderly woman's eyes nearly close inside the laugh lines circling her brow.

As she swallowed hungrily, Un-hee suddenly heard the roar of a boat rushing over the water. Her eyes followed the green cruiser speeding past, slicing a plume of snow out of the sea. The steady whine continued and the vessel was almost out of sight when the engines died and it drifted along the far cliff wall.

They're looking for me, thought Un-hee, and there's nothing there to show them I'm dead. When her eyes returned to her breakfast, she noticed Soo-mee watching her.

"Your eyes are filled with fear, child. Are you in any trouble with the army?" The creases in her forehead furrowed deeper with the question.

"No, sister," Un-hee answered, looking down at her food. "Why would you say that?"

Soo-mee nodded towards the cliff. "Because that's an army boat over there and it seems to be looking for someone."

As Un-hee squinted towards the boat again, the sun's first thin rays sliced through the morning, setting Tiger Island on fire. Its cheeks blushed red and then orange as the sun burnt through some rags of mist still clinging to its walls. The water surrounding it dazzled as though an ocean full of diamonds lapped at its edges. The yellow fire peeked around the cliff at Un-hee and darkened her sight to everything else, warming her cheeks as it kissed her. She turned back to Soo-mee.

"They're looking for me," Un-hee responded quietly.

Soo-mee's eyes looked back at her in love and concern, and in them, Un-hee realized how much she still yearned for her mother. The guidance and acceptance in Soo-mee's worn face had been missing from her life ever since her mother was abducted so many years ago.

"But please don't let them find me," she continued, grabbing Soo-mee's arm. "I ran away from my husband last night and I nearly died. If he finds me now, I really am better off dead. You can't let them know I'm here." Her eyes pled with the elderly diver.

"Shhhh," Soo-mee soothed as she pushed Un-hee's tangled hair back from her forehead. "It's ok, child. I'll make sure you're safe." She held Un-hee's hands in her own calloused palms. "They won't find you with us. But before they start coming back this way, we need to hide you."

She looked around for a guise. "Here," she said, gathering some of her diving gear. "I want you to put a cap and goggles on your head and grab a basket. You're going to be a Jeju diving woman. They won't notice you if you're in the water with us."

Un-hee received the equipment, and gulped down the rest of her breakfast. "But I don't want to get these new clothes all wet too," she said, pulling on her tan shirt.

"We'll leave them here and you can go in those torn rags you have on underneath. Just until the danger is over."

Un-hee removed the brown shirt and pants, along with her new sling, and fitted the linen cap over her head as she followed Soo-mee towards the water. Together, they waded into the morning ocean and held their floating baskets in front of them as they kicked to join the others. Un-hee slipped the goggles over her eyes and stayed close to Soo-mee.

"So where will you go from here, child?" asked Soo-mee when they had reached the other divers. "Do you think you'll be able to avoid the army for long?"

"I don't know," Un-hee sighed, watching the women plunging below and surfacing with their catch. "I have no money and nowhere to go, but I know I must leave Jeju quickly or I will be discovered."

"You have no home?"

"Not anymore. I can never go back to my father's house. He forced me to marry this man and he would push me back to him if he knew I was alive."

Un-hee squinted as the sun floated out of the ocean amid blurring heat waves. She heard the growl of diesel engines and saw the navy craft appear from behind the cliff, splitting the water before a flaming east sky, and hurrying past Tiger Island and across the bay. She hoped the speedboat would return directly to its berth, and, as it drew parallel with the divers, seemed that it would.

Then Un-hee heard a snarl, and the cutter slackened its roar and swung around towards her. She slid deeper into the water and hid behind her float as the rumbling of the army vessel grew, shaking the sea with vibrations. This is it, Un-hee's mind raced. They will pull up, pluck me out of the water, and take me back to him.

She closed her eyes and wished she had stayed in the cave.

eleven

A ceaseless banging at the door wrenched Ju-han from his troubled sleep. He squinted amid the wash of yellow sunshine spilling in through the eastern window. The room was already hot, and the cruel rays stung Ju-han's brain as they pierced the darkness still cloaking his mind from the night before. Ju-han tried to find the source of the noise as the banging continued unabated. Through the front doors, he saw two grim-faced soldiers flanking General Jin in the middle. They were all watching him as one soldier continued striking the glass with his rifle. Ju-han scrambled from bed and unlocked the door, pulling it wide.

"Good morning to you, Mr. Kim. I'm sorry to have to stir you so early," rasped the General. His pocked face stood sullen on the lawn.

"What have you found?" replied Ju-han, rubbing his eyes and scratching his hair.

"We launched a boat to the site about 30 minutes ago, and the men onboard were able to retrieve the hanbok from the rocks. However, we regret to inform you that nothing else was found at the site." The General's complexion seemed made of wood, and the sun flooded every knot and crevice as he spoke into the east.

"Nothing more at all?" Ju-han asked. "Nothing? Are you completely sure?"

"I'm sorry, sir." The General's oak face was unyielding, and the scar on his right cheek looked liked dried sap.

Ju-han stood for a moment in silence. His hands began twitching at his sides, though he was unaware of it. When he did speak, his voice seemed to come from somewhere far away as it squeaked between his teeth: "How could you not find her body?" In a moment, his worst fears from the previous night were ringing a shrill song of reality within his ears.

"As I told you, there was nothing else in the area. But we will continue to search the shore in both directions for any clues. I understand this must be distressing for you, but I assure you, everything humanly possible is being done."

"General, you haven't a hint of what this is like for me." Ju-han lowered his forehead and sharpened his glare. "Last night, I lost the only woman I've ever loved, and now you can't even rescue her body from the cruel sea. You couldn't possibly understand what I'm going through, and unless you find her, you're not doing all you can." Ju-han turned back towards the door when the General gripped his shoulder and stopped him.

"Mr. Kim, I can see you're upset. I have a suggestion: perhaps you'd like to come out with us as we search. It might help you to be part of the rescue effort."

Ju-han stood for a moment and tried to rub away the sleep that still clung to the edges of his eyes. He rested his right hand against his chin and now realized it was shaking on its own. He quickly cupped it with his left hand and replied, "Yes, I think that's a good idea. I will join you."

"Excellent. Come over to the hotel as soon as you're ready and we'll head out." The General turned and marched stiffly away, still pinched between the rifle-bearing escorts.

Ju-han threw his suitcase onto the bed and pulled out a pair of tan shorts and a blue shirt. The fabric felt cool on his skin after sweating through the humidity all night. After dressing, he went to the bathroom and bathed his face and hands in the granite basin, letting the cool water run over them in an attempt to stop their spasms.

He was pulling the door open to leave when he spied Un-hee's suitcase still sitting where he had left it in the darkness by the entrance. Curiosity seized him and he dragged it over to the bed, unzipped it and laid it open. Inside, Un-hee's clothes were folded perfectly, and her shoes and umbrella tucked neatly into the side pouch. Everything was in place except for several crumpled sheets of paper near the top. These Ju-han took and unfolded. Most of them were letters written to Un-hee by her mother when Un-hee was still young. Ju-han sifted through them quickly and was about to throw all of it back into the suitcase when he found a worn letter written by Shin-char, and dated February 22, 1953.

To my beautiful Un-hee,

I long to be with you, my sweet! My eyes are blind without you and my heart bursts for the day that I can see you and hold you in my arms again. I ache for you, my love. You are life to me, and I know that without you, I cannot live. I know I told you my duty was supposed to finish this week but they have re-assigned me. We are going to be part of one more offensive before I can go home. I don't know how long it will be but I promise you that when I arrive, we will be married and I will never leave your side again.

Ever.

I wrote a poem for you in my diary the other day, and I will write it again here. I miss you so much, love.

> *my sun she set 2 years ago,*
> *for darkness enveloped me,*
> *i felt the cold and wind and snow,*
> *gone was my source of heat.*
>
> *without my sun i lose the way,*
> *i can't see cloud from sky,*
> *without my sun i have no day*
> *all blends to one long night.*
>
> *i warm myself with sunny thoughts,*
> *around the fire of memories,*
> *summer sun filled my empty box,*
> *as i passed her my only key.*
>
> *for now my sun must live within,*
> *for darkness cloaks outside,*
> *i look ahead with inward grin,*
> *my sun i shall hold as my bride.*

I hope you like it. Think sunny thoughts, my sun, until I get home and hold you again.

All my love to you, my love

Shin-char

Ju-han stared at the black ink on the paper for a moment before tearing it into strips. He threw the rest of letters back into the suitcase and heaved it off the bed behind him. He recalled how Un-hee had locked the bathroom door last night, and had delayed opening it when he had demanded. Un-hee's words about Shin-char she had uttered during the argument replayed in his mind, and they kindled his rage. The fire within his lungs flared again as he rushed out of the guesthouse, his mind a tortured organ bent on finding his bride, whether dead or alive. He would not be cheated of his possession.

He crossed the lawn standing tall in the morning's rays. The green carpet blushed as its roots drank deep from the night's heavy rainfall. The thick palm trees scattered about still lay long shadows across the dewy carpet, and were crowned with lazy fans wafting in the ocean breeze. As Ju-han reached the hotel doors, he glanced back and couldn't believe how different the entire grounds appeared in the rising sunshine from last night's dark and thieving storm. Even the tall pine trees at the cliff's edge flushed their emerald plumage against the azure sea beyond. A bird fluttered into their midst and whistled a clear-throated song from within their needles. The day had dawned a mockery upon his loss, and Ju-han saw but ghastly rays from the rising sun and heard only a shrill bird calling to no one.

He pushed open the glass door and walked over to the front desk where General Jin stood waiting with several other officers. They bowed slightly to each other and then Jin led him out of the main entrance and into a waiting army truck. The General held the door open, and Ju-han climbed in and sat next to the driver while Jin entered last, sandwiching Ju-han in the middle. After the General had swung the door shut, the truck roared and heaved through the gears, leaving the castle walls behind. Ju-han stared straight ahead, watching as trees bled past and the road was sucked under him in dreamlike vividness.

After bouncing along for a few minutes, the truck lurched onto a small lane bordered on both sides by lava rock fences. These were built by carefully piling stones one on top of the other until they formed a wall. Once in place, they were stable, and perfectly designed to withstand Jeju's powerful winds by allowing the breeze to sieve through the cracks between the rocks. Beyond these volcanic hedges lay tangerine groves on both sides, where orange fruit bobbed amid a sea of green. Each grove was separated from the others by a line of cedar trees standing tall and straight, protecting the fruit from ravishing winds. The lane twisted continually through the groves and split several times, causing Ju-han to soon lose all sense of direction.

As they rounded yet another sharp corner, a butterfly appeared from between the rocks in the fence and flew into the middle of the road. Its wings were the colour of blood bordered with yellow ribbon that gleamed in the sun as it skipped and danced with glee, oblivious to the metal terror bearing down upon it.

Ju-han watched the happy creature and despised its joy. As the truck drew nearer, he wished it flattened against the windshield. The painted wings continued to flutter about until the truck was almost upon it when it flew straight up. Ju-han hoped the top of the cab had struck it, and he watched the side mirrors carefully for any sign of the butterfly. Nothing appeared at first, but after several seconds, the sunlit wings reappeared in the middle of the road, skipping and flitting as before. Ju-han clenched his trembling fists and turned his eyes back onto the road ahead.

The truck finally hissed its arrival at the end of a lane hedged by tangerine fields on all three sides. The three men climbed out, and Ju-han followed the driver and General Jin down a narrow path winding across a field dripping with orange fruit.

"We are going to one of the army outposts we have along the shores of Jeju Island," explained the General as they walked along. "There is a boat waiting for us. We set out from this location earlier this morning when we conducted the initial search." Ju-han nodded silently and kept his eyes forward as ocean waves became visible through the trees ahead.

Soon, they arrived at the shore where a charcoal building hid amid some trees along the edge of the island. Long grass grew from the flat roof of the outpost, making it invisible to any aircraft above, while a tongue of rock thrust out into the ocean just beyond the building and shaped a sheltered cove in front of it. At the water's edge, beside a worn dock, bobbed two green-hulled patrol boats.

Suddenly, one of them gurgled and whined as soldiers sparked it to life. Ju-han climbed in after the General and the craft reversed and swung wide towards the open sea, the engine growling behind them. They rounded the spit of rock and cut into the waves curling down on them from the east. The breeze carried a salty reek of fish into Ju-han's nose and wiped away any sleepy mist still clouding his mind. Seogwipo Harbour appeared on the left cradling a vast army of fishing boats between its two arms of stone. Beyond the seaport, sheer cliffs rose in the distance, their dark foreheads towering far above the water lapping at their feet. Behind, the sky was painted as a wall of gold while on the right stood the high crown of Tiger Island, providing the horizon's only gap in the forever embrace of blue sky and bluer sea.

The harbour slipped past and the cliffs grew ahead. Soon, Ju-han could see the black face of the Sunrise Hotel gazing out from behind a fringe of pine trees on the highest cliff. Only the uppermost turrets were clearly visible above the trees, their windows blushing rose in the climbing sun. He looked left towards the shore and spotted the waterfall emptying itself into the ocean, the very waterfall that had witnessed his frustration at the end of his search last night. He felt again the helplessness he had known there, and gripped the boat's steel railing to calm his quivering hands.

In front of the waterfall, at the bottom of the stone staircase, he saw a crowd of people huddled around a green tarp. Ju-han's gaze drifted over from them and his eye struck upon a dark hole in the rock just below and left of the staircase. An oval-shaped cave burrowed into the cliff barely above sea level, like a black egg lying sideways.

At that moment, the General joined him at the prow.

"See anything interesting?" asked Jin, gripping the side of the boat with both hands and looking towards the shore.

"Not really, I was just looking at that hole in the rock over there." Ju-han pointed toward the shore.

"Oh, yes. That's the end of a lava tube, an interesting feature of Jeju. They were formed at the birth of the island and are steeped in mystery. Have you ever heard anything about them?"

"No, I haven't"

"You should have a look inside one, if you get the chance. They're quite interesting. Legends say the ancient snake gods that lived in them demanded human sacrifices to be appeased. They preferred the lives of young women. And if you listen closely, you might even hear the poor victims' screams crying out from somewhere under the volcano."

Ju-han gave the General a sideways glance and then looked back in the direction of the shore.

"And over there by the waterfall," Jin continued, pointing at the green tarp, "are the diving women of Jeju, selling their catch fresh from the sea. We passed them earlier this morning when they were diving at sunrise."

Ju-han turned from the waterfall and crowd of people to the rocky shoreline drawing near as the boat cut its power and rumbled slowly past the cliff's porous face.

"So how have you been holding up?" asked the General.

"I'm managing ok. I should be able to struggle on as long as I know where my little sparrow is," replied Ju-han, examining the coastline.

"Hopefully we are able to find more clues this time. We will have more light so there's a good chance we might." Without turning his head, the General spied Ju-han from the corner of his eye, and then looked forward again.

"I agree, General."

"Have you been able to think of anything else about last night? Anything at all that might be useful in finding out where she might be?"

"No, I haven't. You know all I do about what happened yesterday and probably more."

"Yes, you did go through everything but sometimes even the smallest detail can uncover hidden possibilities. Like, was your bride wearing anything else besides the hanbok when she went out?"

The General continued to blink straight ahead but had now shuffled closer to Ju-han so that their shoulders nearly touched.

"Well, I would assume she was wearing underwear and whatever else women wear under dresses. I'm not sure I understand what you want from me," Ju-han replied as he peeked over at the General. The scar on his face had turned warm pink in the morning sun.

"It just seems very strange to me that we found the dress so easily, and no other trace of her anywhere around here." The General's right elbow now pressed against Ju-han's arm and did not move away.

"Why is that strange?" Ju-han shot back. "It probably came off her as she was tossed around in the violent waves. You might recall that there was quite a storm last night. And then, because you guys refused to go out immediately, her body was probably taken out to sea by the tide or whatever ocean creatures could get at her."

Ju-han slid away from the General as the engines' gurgling died completely. They drifted along at the cliff's feet, the boat rising and falling as the waves splashed among the boulders before them.

153

"That's a distinct possibility except for a couple things I just thought of," the General rasped in reply.

"And what are those?"

"The storm would have pushed her into shore, not out to sea. And there are very few creatures in these waters large enough to take her body anywhere. But let's put those aside. There's one issue that I find much more puzzling." The General stopped and faced Ju-han directly.

"Yes?"

"The hanbok was completely done up, all the way to the neck, and the bow was knotted tight around it with no way for it to come off her body without tearing open."

The General hesitated.

"And it wasn't torn."

Ju-han quickly turned away towards the cliff. He watched the sable boulders gleaming with saltwater and sunshine as he strained to betray no clue in his face about the hanbok's true nature. He mentally cursed himself for being so careless, and desperately searched for a safe reply.

A young soldier in a black diving suit gave him a reprieve as he approached Jin. "General, we have reached the point of impact and the anchor has been lowered. We await your orders."

General Jin turned to face the soldier while Ju-han glanced at him briefly from over his shoulder, and then resumed weaving his response.

The General gave the sailor instructions and a minute later, two divers fell overboard and began searching the emerald waters directly below the cliff from which Un-hee had plunged just the night before. The sea was clear and they covered the area quickly, circling ever wider away from the boat. Jin had disappeared into the engine room while Ju-han stood unmoved at the prow, watching the divers' progress. The boat was rumbling forward again when the General returned.

"We are going to slide ahead a little bit and see if we can find anything farther up the coastline. We investigated the area leading up to this spot earlier this morning but we stopped our search here." He leaned over the railing to mark the divers' positions. "Maybe the tide has left us some clues."

"That sounds like a good idea, but I fear we'll find nothing," replied Ju-han. "I still think that sharks or something else have already taken her away because the search was not carried out immediately." He rested his head on his forearm against the railing and tried to force tears into his eyes.

"Like I said earlier, Mr. Kim, there's not much in these waters that could have moved her anywhere. Sharks are rarely seen along these coasts, and I can guarantee going out last night would have yielded nothing but needless danger to my men. If your wife actually fell from this cliff, we will find her."

"What are you trying to say, 'if she fell'? You don't believe what I've told you?" Ju-han's stung eyes glared up at the General, and he suddenly forgot all else but this wooden man standing before him.

"Well, I believe that you haven't told me everything. I have yet to hear your explanation of how the hanbok came off your wife's body without being undone and without tearing. And while we're discussing it, how was she able to fall all that distance to these rocks below, and not leave a single blood stain on that dress?" General Jin's searching eyes never left the rocky coastline, but his voice was a metal door slamming in Ju-han's ears.

"These questions are impossible for me to answer, General, because the last time I saw Un-hee, she was walking out of the door of our honeymoon suite. So I'm sorry, I can't help you. But while we are discussing the hanbok, why hasn't it been returned to me yet?"

"It hasn't been returned to you because it never will be. It's been entered as evidence and is the state's property now."

"Evidence? Evidence for what? You can't just take it away like that. It belongs to me."

"It's a crucial piece of physical proof if this investigation happens to change gears. And especially if we cannot find anything else out here."

"Changes gears? I don't understand. What are you trying to say?" asked Ju-han.

"I never try to say anything, and if you don't understand, I can't help you. It's been an interesting conversation, Mr. Kim. We will swing around now and leave you back at the waterfall.

I'm sure you can find your way to the hotel from there. We're going to continue searching here today and we'll keep you informed of any developments. And Mr. Kim, " the General looked directly in Ju-han's eyes and gripped his arm, "don't leave the hotel for any reason. We will let you know when and how you are to leave. Go up and get some rest. I'll be in touch."

Jin bowed slightly and returned to the control room leaving Ju-han alone at the rail. The boat swung about with a growl from the engines and sped around the cliff's face to the waterfall plunging on the other side. The green hull drew alongside the rocks and a board was thrown out to span the water to shore. Ju-han leapt from the plank and landed amid black boulders as the boat roared away, churning a clutch of snowy feathers behind it.

twelve

Only when the vessel was almost upon the divers did its engines roar to life and growl away, dragging a frothing white tail. Un-hee exhaled and climbed back onto her pontoon.

"Looks like you do need to get away fast," said Soo-mee, still watching the boat trail away. "There's one option I can think of that might work. A ship leaves for Busan three times a week at 1:00 pm from the harbour over there." She pointed at a cement wharf thrusting a long grey arm into the ocean with several rope-choked masts swaying behind it. "I believe it sails today."

"That sounds perfect if I had the money," Un-hee replied wistfully, watching the fishing boats busying with the dawning day's work.

Soo-mee was watching Un-hee again when she turned back from the harbour. Un-hee felt vulnerable under the woman's gaze, as though the wrinkled face saw much more than just her eyes and skin. When Soo-mee looked at her, Un-hee knew it was her soul she saw. Though she resisted, Un-hee could easily have told Soo-mee her entire life history and she would have felt like she was telling an old story to somebody who already knew the outcome. She was comfortable with her, and felt like she could trust her with her life. Soo-mee trapped her eyes inside her goggles and adjusted the strap around her head, still looking at Un-hee. Then she dove beneath the water without a word.

Un-hee watched the other diving women taking turns bubbling through the surface to deposit crabs, clams, sea slugs, abalone, and various other offerings into their baskets. She marveled at their strength and ability to dive for such long periods without air. Soo-mee still hadn't surfaced yet when Un-hee began swimming back towards shore. The sea has held me in its unloving arms long enough for one day, she thought.

Emerging from the ocean, she spied a tangle of hedge growing along the cliff face. Behind this cover, she removed her ripped pajamas and stepped back into the stiff shirt and brown pants. Their fabric felt similar to the clothes her mom and grandma had worn when they had toiled long days in the fields behind their house. Un-hee folded her silk pajama pants and wondered where she could hide them for nobody to find.

She was bundling the shirt, wishing there was a fire nearby that could devour them, when her fingers closed around the picture she had hid there in haste just last night.

So long ago.

She pulled it out and slumped down on the stony beach with her back against a boulder. She held the faded faces between her fingers and wept again at her mother's memory. How much she had yet to live and do when those evil soldiers came to take her away, she thought. How much love and affection she had still to give. And how much more did she leave untaught within me.

Sitting on that rocky shore, Un-hee made a vow to herself: any child I have will know me until she has learned all that I can teach her about life. A mother's touch can never be replaced. And the more Un-hee looked at her grandma's wrinkled face in the picture, the more resemblance she saw between it and Soo-mee.

She tucked the picture into her pocket and looked out to sea. The women continued their foraging as the sun rose higher and spread more of its hot face over the surface of the sea. On land, nothing hid from its heat; but beneath the ocean's flat complexion sang a world unwearied by the sun's fickle passes. An aquatic garden filled with a thousand varieties of crops spread in every direction, and Un-hee watched as the aged gardeners diving before her harvested their plot.

She sat on the beach, thankful to be dry and fed, and watched the distant horizon change colours and don its daytime hues. Her thoughts wafted with the morning's light breeze, twisting and circling through the past night's harrowing events until they settled again on Ju-han. Un-hee's soul ached at his memory as though bleeding from wounds that would never close. His cruelty still tore her inside and made her wish that he had been the one to plunge from the cliff in her place, only onto stone to match the substance of his heart.

She also wished that the black fog of his family had never darkened her shores. Every great evil she had ever known had been a direct result of Ju-han and his family. Now that she was finally free of him, she was forced to live as dead to the rest of the world. She could never remain on Jeju Island, nor return to the life she had known. Her home, her friends, her father were all dead to her if she wished to remain free. Too many people would hear of her death, and Ju-han would never end his quest to find her, especially if he hears that she lives. Even beyond death's thin threshold, his dark webs spread around her and bound her to his power. Through their black strands, the sun managed only a pale beam of yellow that seemed blotchy and weak to Un-hee's eyes.

As she sat enveloped in gloom, Soo-mee and the other divers emerged from the ocean, their dripping suits gleaming as black leather buffed to a shine by the sun behind them. They walked up to Un-hee and stood in front of her, chasing away the darkness cloaking her mind.

Soo-mee bent low and looked in her face. "We have decided to help you further in your journey, child. If you would like to take the boat, we will give you all the money this catch brings in. It should carry you as far as Busan at least." Her lined face split with a smile. Un-hee looked from her to the others and saw that all the diving women surrounding her were grinning and nodding their heads. A flood rose in Un-hee's throat and leaked from her eyes.

"Thank you so much, sisters," she cried, blinking through her tears. "Thank you so much for your kindness."

"We will set up our area near the waterfall over there and we should have most of this sold by 11:00," Soo-mee continued. "Tourists usually come down early to snap it up. Then afterwards, I can escort you to the ship and see you off to happier shores."

"Thank you again with all my heart."

"You are a beautiful flower, child, but a bruised one. We will do our best to care for you and bring you back to health. You have much good yet to accomplish in this world."

The diving women gathered their equipment and moved everything back up the beach. Un-hee followed behind them carrying her pajamas under her arm. As she walked among the boulders, every step closer to the hotel laid another chain over her heart. By the time the waterfall was again plunging in her ears, she carried a shackled stone between her lungs.

She began helping the women set up their operation. A green cloth was stretched between four poles to shield the women from the sun, and two large tubs were filled to the brim, one with seawater and another with freshwater from the waterfall. Emptying their baskets into the saltwater tub, the diving women settled into place on flat stones and began preparing the seafood.

Un-hee sat on the rock-hewn steps and watched the cascading water crash into the pool spread at her feet. Before long, early risers from the hotel were descending the stairs to gaze at the waterfall and the diving women. Many ordered plates of assorted sea delicacies served with side dishes of chopped garlic and the famous red pepper paste. The women were as much an attraction as the food, and the crowd grew steadily and flocked around them as they worked in orchestrated rhythm, each member a vital link to the resulting gourmet.

Un-hee approached Soo-mee. "I think I'll go wait somewhere quieter," she whispered as the diving woman was slicing some abalone.

"Sure, child. I'll come find you when it's time."

Un-hee slipped away from the throng and walked over to the lava tube, still carrying her pajamas under her arm. Here I'll be hidden from the heat and the people, she mused. She climbed back into the low cave and felt its musty coolness on her face. The throat of the tunnel sank into deepest black, and Un-hee had to grope along while her eyes adjusted. Soon, she stumbled over her rock pillow sitting in the middle of the floor. Not far enough, she thought. She wanted to retreat deep into the cave, wanted to bury herself from probing fingers and eyes. As she crept along, she turned frequently to measure her progress with the shrinking oval doorway behind. At one such instance, she looked back and saw another navy boat out on the ocean in front of Tiger Island, slicing back towards the same cliff. She was relieved that a mantle of cool lava covered her while it roamed outside.

She took several more steps and discovered she had reached the cave's elbow where it hooked to the left, abandoning the fraction of light that snuck up the tunnel to this point. She sat on the floor of stone with her pajamas underneath her and watched the oval disc of ocean shimmer in a black cauldron. Her eyes stung when she blinked and she felt spent from the previous night's exhaustion. She soon slipped into a sound rest.

Scraping noises echoing through the tube awoke her. She opened her eyes and saw a black figure set against the gleaming sea clambering into the cave! Un-hee sat unmoved as it climbed into the tunnel and stopped, groping around with its hands. Sinking to the floor, it looked like a crouching bear ready to lunge. A wet shiver slid over Un-hee's skin and every sense told her to flee this intruder.

She rose to her feet and backed away slowly from the elbow's kink. Then she spotted her silk pants and shirt still lying on the cave floor. Easing forward, she silently retrieved them as the dark figure yet hunched in the middle of the tunnel's doorway. The oval monocle of light slid from view as Un-hee retreated deeper again and blackest ink enveloped her. She backed still further, then turned and shuffled as quietly as she could deeper into the island's belly.

She couldn't go far. Only seven steps from the turn, she stumbled into a wall of boulders choking the tunnel. She probed the slimy rocks with her hands but could find no gap anywhere. Thousands of years before, the roof had caved in, clogging the lava tube with tons of broken stone. She was trapped.

Her terrifying dream replayed in her mind as she shrunk down into a corner, wedging her back between the wet wall and a slimy boulder. Only this time, the wave was a stationary wall of stone behind, and the tiger an unknown figure advancing towards her. With her arms, she clasped her knees against her chest and listened to the shuffling growing louder in the tube. She could see a vague shadow gesturing on the wall at the tunnel's elbow; the image swelled and its edges sharpened as the figure drew nearer. Soon it resembled the tiger of her dream, lumbering towards her with claws spread wide and a man's head rolling on immense shoulders.

In the next instant, the person rounded the corner and hit his head against the shadow wall, wincing from pain. It was smaller than its shadowy likeness, and wore light shorts and a dark shirt. Un-hee immediately recognized the clothes, and knew the voice to be Ju-han's!

Her heart stopped and her stomach closed in on itself. She became like the rock that surrounded her as she watched Ju-han stumble and then fall to his knees in the darkness beyond the corner. She heard him growl again from striking his head, and his breath swept over her in waves of vapour. Though he was completely shrouded in blackness, Un-hee felt like he was close enough to reach out and grab her. She held her breath as he groaned.

Suddenly, she heard him take a step. The noise sounded nearer and startled her as a mountain-high squeal fled through her teeth. He's coming for me!

thirteen

Ju-han watched the stern curl out of view behind the cliff wall. The sun had already scaled high into the blank sky and its hot face lit the hunger and fatigue he carried inside. He now saw that the people huddled around the green tarp were early morning tourists, and he could smell the delicate aroma of seafood wafting out from their midst. The crowd praised the fresh scallops, shellfish, abalone, and sliced octopus that the aged diving women were preparing, and, as Ju-han listened nearby, he caught a hint of chopped garlic and red pepper paste passing in the sea breeze, and his mouth watered with every scent.

He was about to hike the stone stairway to the guesthouse and retrieve some money when he remembered the cave he had seen from the boat, lurking somewhere west of the waterfall. He decided to take a quick glance inside it before rushing away for breakfast cash.

Stepping from one boulder to another while the ocean slid under him, Ju-han carefully examined the shoreline. A low brow of rock frowned beneath heavy vines and leaves groping down from above. The lava stone was a black blanket full of scars, frozen into writhing shapes of agony and molten fury. When he had explored a little farther down the cliff wall, he found the snake's lair yawning beneath a lip of hardened lava. He crouched inside.

As soon as he passed the entrance, Ju-han was blinking into utter darkness since his eyes had yet to adjust from the morning's radiance. Turning, he looked out to sea from his pigeon hole, and Tiger Island beyond was centered perfectly in its oval frame. As he waited for his pupils to dilate, he sat on a round rock lying in the middle of the lava tube. The floor was remarkably flat and smooth as though water had swept away the splintered edges through many dark years. But very little water now dribbled in the ridges beneath Ju-han's shoes, and he marveled at the width and preciseness of this natural phenomenon. As his eyes were able to further pierce the never-ending night within this hole, he imagined a river of liquid stone, flowing through an underground tunnel eons ago and freezing like glass, sealing itself to its course.

The General was right, he thought. This really is fascinating.

Crouching, Ju-han shuffled as far into the cave as he dared, turning often to see how small the plate of ocean behind him had shrunk. The air was musty and smelled of dripping moss and rock. Ju-han disliked touching the wet walls, especially when the tunnel turned to the left and he stumbled into some barbs sticking out from the right side of the cave.

One pointed edge cut into his temple and, when he winced from the pain, he could hear his exclamation tumbling down the tunnel behind him. Kneeling to the ground, he gently probed the wound and felt warm blood trickling down his fingers and into his hand. He looked into the new direction the tube had chosen and wondered if his eyes were open at all. The night lurking in the tunnel beyond this point was thicker than ink; nothing filled his vision so entirely that he was unable to notice a difference between having his eyes open or keeping them closed.

Slowly, he rose to his feet and decided to return to daylight. When he took the first returning step, he heard what sounded like a shrill cry echo behind him.

Ju-han froze on the spot. He was so stunned and frightened that he couldn't move. His heart burst from his chest, sending blood pounding past his ears in furious rhythm, and his mind raced over the General's words about the snake gods' victims.

Are they crying out at me? Am I intruding on holy ground? Then his panicked brain thought of his bride. Did Un-hee's spirit flee into this cave when she died? Is her blood screaming my name? Maybe she joined with the ancient ghosts and they're all coming to lynch me! Ju-han's ribs quivered inside while he stood as still as stone and waited, listening even with his skin.

Petrified, Un-hee held her knees to her chest. After her cry had escaped down the tunnel, a silence of death flooded in; nothing moved. The absence of noise was so complete that it hung as a deafening fog between the two blind souls. She waited a seeming eternity and still Ju-han didn't move; he didn't even breathe. Un-hee's lungs were shriveled from want of air before she heard his first tentative step.

Ju-han waited, but no sound came. No second haunted cry, not even a drip of water broke the silence. Seconds crept by him as his back and legs started to ache from the spring-loaded stillness; he pulled his breath in so slowly that it hardly reached his lungs. And still no sound came.

Slowly, finally, he relaxed. His mind, seeking solace, conceived that a pebble scraped by his shoe against the stone floor had sent an odd squeak bouncing misshapen through the tunnel and had returned to his ears as a cry. However, he couldn't wash away the thought of ancient ghosts lamenting from inside the volcano, and he was still trapped in their underground lair, in the throat of the spirits. He would take no liberties until he was safe in his own world of daylight.

Cautiously, Ju-han stepped his left foot forward and all was quiet. He peeked around the corner of stone: the mouth of the tunnel was an island of blue and gold floating amid a sea of coal. It warmed his eyes to see it.

She was still unsure in which direction he was moving until he took his second step and was washed in the pale gleam from the entrance. Without turning back, he shuffled faster and faster down the corridor. Un-hee remained bound to the floor until she was sure he was flying from the cave.

He took another step, and, when no strange sound followed, he started walking faster, one foot shuffling past the other in anxious rhythm. He was determined to fly from the cave before any spirits from the underworld could sink their unseen teeth into his neck.

She stood and peeked around the corner. He had almost reached the entrance and was moving faster than ever. He's actually scared, she thought. My squeak scared him. He never knew I was in the tunnel too. She sucked in a lungful of air and released her shrillest scream, sending it tearing down the tunnel with chilling force.

Ju-han was near the entrance when he heard it again. The cry was louder this time, and pierced his ears like a sharpened needle. Yet it seemed to come from a chorus of throats, and from far away like an echo at the bottom of a deep well. No pebble had scraped the floor beneath his foot this time; he knew the wail was real.

"Not me!" he screamed at the ghosts, running hunched over as fast as he could towards the doorway. "Leave my neck alone!" His feet moved as though in glue, and his back ached with every step. The golden plate of sunlight shone before him as he slid as fast as he could towards it.

Ju-han burst from the stone tomb and kneeled before the ocean exhausted. He inhaled deeply for several minutes at the water's edge, staring into the round pebbles under his trembling hands while his back heaved with breath. Turning around, he looked back at the black eye staring from the rock and shook in fear.

This is the beginning of my torment, he thought, the word burning in his mind. I have set in motion events that otherwise would not have happened. Somehow, I know I had a hand in Un-hee's death. I know if I had not been in her life, she would still be alive today. I can see that now, and I believe it. My punishment draws near.

After his breathing settled down, he stood and picked his way back towards the waterfall, delighted to smell the sea and feel the sun's warm glow on his face again. Being outside in mundane surroundings once again made him feel a bit ridiculous about his hysteria in the tunnel, and he rolled his shoulders and stretched his neck, hoping to turn the shrieks in his head into just another vivid hallucination.

Stepping over waterlogged boulders, Ju-han climbed up to where the diving women still prepared their delicacies next to the thundering waterfall. The crowds of tourists had not thinned, and continued to indulge themselves in the fruits of the sea and marvel at the skill and strength of the women.

Ju-han was faint with hunger after his ordeal in the lava tube, and he no longer wanted to detour all the way up to the guesthouse to fetch his money. Digging through the people, he approached one of the aged divers. "How much for a plate?" he asked.

"10,000 won," smiled the wrinkled grandmother, gouging the flesh out of a shellfish with her little finger.

"I'll take two, but I can only pay you later. My money is up in my room in the hotel."

"I'm sorry, but we'll need the money right away. We are taking up a special collection for one of our sisters with this…"

"I will pay you!" Ju-han cut her off. "Don't worry about that. I'm starving and I would like to eat right now."

The woman continued cleaning the shellfish. "I'm sorry, sir. You will have to…"

Ju-han jumped in again. "Listen, gramma. I'm hungry now. After I get my food, I will run up there and straight back down with your precious money."

The tourists near Ju-han stepped back when they heard his rant, and murmured about his lack of respect.

Meanwhile, the diving woman's weathered cheeks and bright eyes looked up, watching Ju-han for a moment before she replied. "I'm sorry, these are special circumstances today. Please come back when you have money."

Ju-han stormed up the stone steps, muttering curses at the waterfall.

By the time he stepped into the hedged hotel grounds, he was wheezing and his stomach gnarled in a fit of hunger. His head swirled in confusion, and he felt like he needed to lie down before he fell down. As he stumbled up the path leading to his suite, he found two soldiers in green uniforms waiting for him, sandwiching the glass doors between them. They held automatic rifles at their sides and their eyes stared out from under black helmets.

"What are you guys doing here?" he asked, groping his pockets for the room key.

"We are here on orders for your safety, Mr. Kim," the acne-scarred soldier on the left announced.

"My safety?" Ju-han forced a staccato laugh. "What could possibly be dangerous to me here?" he asked, sliding the key into the lock.

"We are here only as a precaution," the soldier replied, keeping his eyes forward.

"You mean you're here to keep me under a lens," Ju-han shot back, pulling the door open. He turned and stared from one soldier to the other as they both remained motionless beside his doorway. "Leave! Go, right now!"

They appeared to have not even heard him.

"If you are supposed to be here, I want General Jin to come here himself and explain this to me. Otherwise, I will not be caged like a rat. Go!" Ju-han yelled in rage.

The two soldiers remained as still as stone, neither moving nor speaking. Ju-han glared at them in frustration, then slammed the door. Stomping over to the bed, he collapsed on it, closed his eyes, and felt the room spinning in one direction and his body spinning in the other. When he looked up again, the swirling ceiling pattern above slowed and stopped. His life had shattered when Un-hee had fallen from that cliff; gathering the broken pieces was like picking crystal shards from a glass mountain. And, to make his life even more miserable, the General hounded at his heels thinking him a murderer. With no alibi to give, and being the only witness to the death left him with little chance of hiding from suspicion, and he knew that. The General's pursuit would be unforgiving and he would suffer for it, probably many years in an iron cage.

Ju-han needed an escape, a way out. He decided to look for one in the same place he always had whenever he needed to duck responsibility.

He sat up on the bed, reached for the black receiver sitting in its cradle, and asked the front desk clerk to connect him to a number. After several seconds, a hard voice burst in his ears.

"Hello?"

"Hi Dad, it's me."

"My son! How are you? How's married life treating you?"

175

"Dad, my life has fallen apart. There's been a tragedy, a horrible…" Ju-han's voice fell away and only breath left his lips. His throat tightened and he felt like he would choke.

"What is it? What's happened?" his father asked.

"Un-hee's gone, Dad. I think she's dead," and for the first time since his bride had plunged into the churning ocean, Ju-han felt the cold stab of loss in his heart, and thought how beautiful it would be to have Un-hee alive and in his arms again.

"How? Tell me what happened."

Ju-han related to his dad the same scenario he'd told the army, the clerk, and everyone else. He made sure to include only the details that were commonly known thinking that if there were to be an inquiry, at least his father wouldn't have to lie about anything he knew. As Ju-han spoke, his mind increasingly accepted his fabricated details as fact, and any mists of doubt seemed to burn up in the hot stream of sunshine flooding through the window behind him. His heart sunk deeper into his chest and hid beneath his ribs as a black fog shrouded it from light. His body numbed to all that surrounded him. He had to believe: Un-hee was gone from him forever.

"But I know Jin thinks I killed her, Dad. He's after me, there's no doubt. He hounds my steps; he even put two soldiers outside my suite to make sure I wouldn't try to sneak out of the hotel. What should I do?"

"Well, son, are you innocent?" His father's voice carried neither accusation nor condescension; it simply posed a logical question to the circumstances.

"You know I am."

"Then you've got nothing to worry about."

"It's not like that, don't you see? Innocence has absolutely nothing to do with it. I look and smell and taste guilty. It doesn't matter that I'm innocent, Dad. I have no alibi. There are no witnesses. I'm the last person on earth to see her alive, and she's not here to defend me."

"Don't worry about all that right now, son. Just try to relax and think clearly. Why don't you come stay with us for a while and I'll help you sort all this out?"

"I'd love to, Dad, but Jin told me I need to stay here until he lets me leave, which will probably be a few more days. With soldiers crawling behind every corner, I don't have much choice."

"This Jin, is he a General?"

"Yeah, how'd you know?"

"Are his eyes pulled close together and he has a scar on one cheek?"

"That's him. You know him?"

"I did. We were in the army together a long time ago. We served in the same company during the time of liberation from the Japanese. I remember him well, in fact, I don't think I could ever forget him."

"Hey, there's our solution, Dad!" Ju-han exclaimed with glee. "That's how you can get me out of here! General Jin is leading the investigation. Just have a chat with your old army buddy, pull a few strings and I'm free to go."

Silence bled from the other end. Ju-han heard a nasal sigh, then more silence. Finally, his father spoke. "Ju-han, he hates me. I was involved in something many years ago that I've regretted ever since. I never spoke of it to anyone, and I never will, not for anything. He knows some of what I did, and it seems like he also knows that you're my son. I believe that's why he's jumped at the chance to lead the investigation, and that's also why he's concentrating on you so heavily. He tried for a long time to get me, but I always protected myself. Now it looks like he's found a perfect opportunity to hurt me through you. If there's anything about you to exploit, son, anything at all, he will find it and use it against you. He's as unrelenting as a shark when he's smelled blood."

Ju-han's jet eyes bounced from the floor to the window to the small table next to him. His body bristled with the blood racing through it in the death-still heat of the room while hunger twisted his stomach between its jaws and meal time had yet to arrive. His clothes below him drained of their colours, and his hair felt waxy above on his head. The walls boxing him in seemed to be made of steel and concrete while bars grilled his windows and looked out upon the other inmates wandering the fenced yard. Two armed guards stood rigid at the door of his cell.

"Is there nothing you can do to help me?" he whimpered into the mouthpiece.

"I will try, son. I will do all I can from this end. Watch to see what Jin does next, and call me when you have more news. Above all, guard your tongue as a jewel, and avoid Jin as much as you can because he will try to deceive you into saying something he can use against you. Write down all you remember telling him and everyone else you talked to about last night."

"I will, Dad. Thanks."

Ju-han dropped the phone into its steel cradle and wiped the pearls of sweat dotting his forehead. His shirt clung to his shoulders and back like a soaked rag while hunger pangs gnawed at the walls of his stomach. He needed food and time to think, and decided to search for a quiet corner in the hotel where he could find both. As he pulled open the door, the rifles crossed before him righted, and he passed between the two soldiers.

"Still on duty, eh boys? Make sure the place doesn't get away on you while I'm gone."

He left the guards behind and walked around the corner of the suite, stopping as soon as he was out of sight. In the shade beside the stone wall, he waited for several moments and then slowly peered out from behind the corner. The acne-scarred soldier was already breathing into his radio while the other soldier stood rigid beside him. Ju-han slipped back and continued walking towards the hotel.

The sun's blanketing heat seemed to ignite the very air that hung humid along the seacoast. Out towards the ocean, the horizon hid behind a white haze, even blurring Tiger Island to a ghostly outline. Ju-han reached the glass doors and pulled them open. Stepping inside, he crept behind the fountain and along the edge of the marble foyer, avoiding eye contact with everyone who happened nearby. He soon reached the restaurant in the west wing and snuck out to a table on the verandah, tucked beneath an umbrella and a spreading palm tree.

In a few minutes, he had kimchi rice and a bowl of seaweed soup steaming before him, as well as a sweating glass of orange juice. As he speared his food with metal chopsticks and swallowed hungrily, he didn't notice the rotund shadow of Colonel Cho approaching until it shrouded the entire table.

"Well, there's the lucky groom. Did you find your runaway bride yet?" laughed the heavy man with shaking jowls.

"No, Colonel," Ju-han answered coldly. "They fear she's dead."

"Oh no, Ju-han! I'm so sorry. I would never have joked if I … I'm so sorry. What happened? How are you doing?" Behind his square glasses, his eyes were huge and they widened even more with surprise. He settled into the seat opposite Ju-han and eclipsed most of the horizon visible from the secluded corner table.

"They're still speculating but they believe she fell from the cliffs just beyond those trees," Ju-han pointed across the lawn with the tips of his chopsticks. "They found a break in the barrier there that I'm told was intact before last night. The army has searched the shoreline and water in both directions but all they found so far was her hanbok."

"That's tragic," lisped the Colonel, and then blew through his parted lips as his brow rippled with concern. "Hey, are you ok? What happened to your forehead?"

"Oh, that's nothing," Ju-han answered, looking into his soup. "I just got scratched by some branches when I was looking for her last night. You know, it's good to have an old friend like you here in a time like this," continued Ju-han, slurping the broth. "I feel so alone, so desperate. But you know, Colonel, at first I didn't think she was dead. I actually felt like she was still alive, like she was still here somewhere. I sometimes feel that even now."

"That's normal, son. When you lose someone so close, that person seems to carry on within you."

"Not that way, Colonel. I had a thought last night that she might have actually survived the fall, that she didn't die at all." At that moment, a butterfly with painted wings of crimson and gold flittered onto the empty table beside them. Ju-han watched it land and slowly stretch its wings. "I just wish I knew where she was so I could know the truth."

"I understand. Not having a definite answer must be torment. You know, just as that butterfly landed, I remembered that I saw her last night after you had left. Remember? In the west wing?"

"Oh, right! I had forgotten all about that. What exactly happened? I wasn't able to hear the whole story," Ju-han replied, still watching the butterfly.

"Well, it honestly is a bit fuzzy because I was quite tipsy by then, but I remember seeing her on the opposite side of the buffet table I was sampling at the time. I was struck by her appearance because her hair was dripping with water, but was still pinned up high on her head, and her beautiful white hanbok was completely soaked. And she just stood there, unmoving. I spoke to her but she didn't respond. And as I watched, her eyes blazed directly through mine for several seconds, then she turned around and disappeared into the crowd of people. I thought maybe she was angry with me, and then, when I saw you in a frantic state a few minutes later, I thought you must have had a lovers' quarrel. I guess I couldn't have been more wrong."

"What did you say she was wearing?"

"A hanbok. I'm sure it was her wedding hanbok."

Ju-han sat staring at the Colonel and then looked down at the leftover rice on his empty plate. He tried to work through the details but couldn't fit any of it together with what he knew to be true.

"You really did have quite a bit to drink though, didn't you, Colonel?" Ju-han questioned, not looking up from the table.

"That's true, I did. But I remember her clearly. It was as though a fog lifted while she was there, like I became sober for those few seconds. I would bet my life that I saw her last night beside that buffet table. In fact, I'd bet your life."

Ju-han reached for the glass of orange juice and, trembling, drained what was left. As he placed it back on the table, his eyes rested on the butterfly still poised next to him. Suddenly, it took to the air and, without wavering, flew directly at Ju-han's face before veering upwards, around the umbrella and into the tops of the trees.

"Those damn butterflies are everywhere," he grumbled, swinging at it as it flew past.

The Colonel watched it disappear into the branches. "I've never seen that kind before. It's a truly beautiful one." His gaze settled down again. "Ju-han, I'm sorry if I've disturbed you with any of this. You have a lot to deal with right now and I'm probably just making things worse."

"No, Colonel, it's good for me to hear what you saw. It's good to know. I just don't see how it fits in with everything, that's all." He leaned forward and rubbed his eyes. "What I need right now is some familiarity around me because everything is so chaotic in my mind. I've lost my bride and I've gained new enemies."

"Really? Who?"

"Well, the army is leading an investigation into everything right now, and a General named Jin is heading it. Have you heard of him?"

"I don't think so…" The Colonel's lisp hung in the still air for a moment. His eyes widened and his thick eyebrows lifted in interest.

A flutter of caution passed over Ju-han's heart, as though he were being led somewhere he didn't want to go, and his father's caution echoed in his head. Ju-han looked down again at his empty plate, and then pushed it aside. "He's the one heading the investigation, but I don't know too much about him. I've only talked to him a couple of times so far."

"And you feel he's your enemy?"

"Oh no, not him."

"Well, who have you gained as an enemy?" pressed the Colonel.

Ju-han exhaled slowly. "Me. I blame myself a million different ways for what happened and I'd do anything to take back that night and have Un-hee here again."

"You shouldn't blame yourself, son. There's nothing more you could have done. You did all that was possible. Now I wish I had chased after her when I saw her by that table. It would have saved all this agony."

"You didn't know, Colonel. You had no way of knowing. But I really have to be going. Sorry to cut you short, I just have too much on my mind and I need to be alone right now." Ju-han pushed away from the table and stood up.

"I completely understand, my son. My heart goes out to you. Don't hesitate to see me if you need an ear to listen, or a shoulder for support. I'll be here for at least a few more days with the other officers." The Colonel straightened and reached out his hand. Ju-han held its fleshy warmth in his and shook it, though reluctantly in his heart.

"Thanks, Colonel. That's kind of you."

Ju-han walked down the steps and off the verandah, crossing the yard towards the side of the hotel as the Colonel's eyes held steady on his back and narrowed.

fourteen

Un-hee waited in darkness for what seemed at least another hour after Ju-han had fled from the cave. She wanted to be certain he was not around when she finally emerged. Groping around on the stone floor, she found her pajamas, and decided there was no safer place to leave them than this recess inside the island's heart. She shoved them as far as she could into a gap between two rocks in the barrier, leaving them as the last remnant of her life with Ju-han. Satisfied, she crept forward and curled up near the entrance to the cave, watching the rocky coast for the first sign of Soo-mee.

Soon, the elderly diver came walking along the shoreline, hunched over with her hands clasped together behind her back. Un-hee climbed out of the lava tube into the hot brilliance, and started crossing the beach to join her.

"What time is it?" she called across the boulders.

"11:10," Soo-mee answered, looking at the cave entrance. "That's a pretty good hiding spot if you don't want to be seen."

"But it almost wasn't good enough, sister," she replied. "Ju-han nearly trapped me in there."

The elderly woman's eyes widened with concern as Un-hee approached. "Really? He was down here? Are you ok?"

Un-hee stepped gingerly over the rocks and joined Soo-mee beside the lapping waves. "I'm fine now. Yes, he came in there and almost all the way to the end. At first I thought he was coming for me, but it turned out he never knew I was in there at all. He came within a few steps of my huddled body, but thankfully the darkness hid me, and he turned around without ever knowing I was there."

"My child, that was much too close. We have to get you away from here quickly." Soo-mee led her down the shore in the direction of the harbour.

When they had hurried for some distance, Soo-mee slowed the pace and asked, "Tell me, child, what does this man look like?"

"Well, he has thick, black hair usually combed to the side or straight back, piercing eyes, a flat nose that's kind of wide, and pretty dark skin. Today, he was wearing light-coloured shorts and a blue or black shirt, I couldn't tell which. Oh yeah, and he has a gap between his two front teeth. I used to stare at it all the time when he talked."

"I recognize him!" burst Soo-mee. "That's the very same guy who came over to our tent and wanted some food for free. He became rude and irritated when I told him he would have to pay. He didn't look poor so I thought he could afford it."

"He can afford it," answered Un-hee. "He can afford anything he wants. He's so rich and spoiled, and probably just too lazy to go up and get his money." She turned a look back at the hotel perched above the cliff in the distance. "Did you see which way he went?"

"Up the stairs towards the hotel. Hopefully that's the last you ever see of him."

"I hope so too, sister."

They walked together along the beach for a while. Then Soo-mee turned north into a tiny path that twisted up from the ocean, snaking beneath tall trees that spread their leafy arms in worship to the sun. Rock faces watched on both sides until the women had climbed above the bluffs and into the dense forest spread wide on both sides. On every tree's ashen skin hung locusts singing their melody so loudly a deafening chatter rose and fell throughout the wood as Un-hee continued to walk in Soo-mee's steps up the trail.

The path brought them to a road bordered on both sides by lava rock fences. Soo-mee turned west on the road and the two women walked side by side between the balanced stones that marked the edges of tangerine fields. Soo-mee began humming as they marched beneath the scorching sun, and soon the duet was harmonizing to "Arirang" and other old songs that had carried many wearied souls through the dark decades of Japanese occupation. The songs brought Un-hee's mother back to her as this sea-spun and sun-dried grandmother walking beside her sang them just as her mother had when Un-hee was a young girl.

She glanced over at her while they sang, and saw dignity and beauty: Soo-mee's face was safe, and her eyes, when she smiled at Un-hee, watched over her and held her close. Soo-mee reached out and linked her arm through Un-hee's, and the two skipped along the farmers' roads, relishing the day. Un-hee sensed youthful energy in the elderly woman's gait, and the power in her voice trembled through her own arm and body; she felt life coursing into her spirit, and knew she had left death behind. This woman fed her soul. Suddenly, the day seemed brighter, the sunlight more dazzling and the air more fragrant. The tangerines on either side hung like globs of gold from emerald arms stretched out towards the sky. Cedars stood at attention between the fields, licking up sunshine and throwing down pools of shade for the women as they skipped past. Un-hee looked ahead and saw the road they were traveling might actually stretch beyond today into tomorrow, and a following tomorrow, and the chains which had bound her so tightly were snapping beneath the weight of love.

"Have you ever lost anyone close to you?" Un-hee asked as they rounded yet another corner. Before them, the road tumbled down a hill, and below it lay the white harbour, hiding a tangle of boats between its crooked arms.

"When you reach my age, child, you're a rare one not to have lost many dear friends and family. I'm sure we all have, especially considering the times we live in. Why do you ask, child?"

"My mom was taken away when I was seven years old, and later I heard that she had died. I still miss her so much, I think about her everyday. After she was taken, my grandmother died a short while later because the grief was too much for her. But now, since I met you, I find that you help me remember her. You remind me so much of how my mother used to be."

"Oh, my child! No one should have to endure a tragedy like that, not so young. How was she taken from you?"

Un-hee related her memories of that dreadful day: the Japanese soldiers, the guns and the truck, her father's beating. And the screaming, the awful screaming. The cries still rang in her ears as though they had just been uttered.

"How horrible, child," Soo-mee replied when Un-hee had finished. "That's terrible. I wish I had known you then. I would have tried to help you through such pain."

"You already have, sister. You've been a saviour to me already. Since the moment I met you, you've been helping me through it."

She turned to Un-hee and smiled. Then her grin faded, and her face lined with pain. "I also lost several close friends to those vile Japanese camps. 'Comfort stations' they called them. More like killing stations. Most women died in the cruelty, but some made it back after the end of the war. But those poor souls were never the same again. Most of them wouldn't speak of it, and still won't. The few horrors I've heard…" Soo-mee's voice trailed off as her lips tightened. "There aren't words to describe the hell they endured. But those are the atrocities of war. You never know what it's like until you live through it, and then you wish you never had."

Un-hee nodded her head in agreement. They continued in silence for a while before Un-hee spoke again. "You're right, sister. Wars are always better never to have started in the first place. But in a way, I think enduring what I did and suffering through it gave me strength and determination inside. Otherwise, maybe I never would have had the will to leave Ju-han."

"That's possible, child. How long were you married to him?"

"Our wedding was…" So much had happened that Un-hee couldn't believe they were married only yesterday. "Yesterday," she answered in surprise.

"Yesterday?" Soo-mee echoed. "So this was your honeymoon? Last night was your wedding night?"

"Yes, it was." Un-hee paused and then continued. "But no longer. My married existence is buried under that cliff in those angry waves. This is my new life now. I will not wear any man's chains anymore," she announced, rubbing her neck lightly.

"What happened? How did you get away?" Soo-mee asked.

Un-hee looked over at Soo-mee and saw again the clear eyes that hid nothing, and asked for nothing in return. She trusted Soo-mee, possibly more than she trusted anyone else alive, and she knew any words passed to her would be kept safe, and would never be divulged to anyone.

Un-hee took a deep breath and related the entire story to her, omitting nothing. She started in her father's tangerine orchard, in the carefree days with Shin-char and her mother, amid rainy afternoons, and cold winter winds. Her heart swelled with the memories, and her words sang happily from her lips. Then came the abduction of her mother by Japanese forces, as directed by Ju-han's father, and her grandmother's death that left her alone and fearful with her father. Her turmoil through her early teen years swirled together in a dark and confusing fog, punctuated by her father's rages.

Un-hee's speech now sank slow and heavy through her teeth.

Her single joy, her only ray of light during that time had come from Shin-char, from his unwavering devotion and trust. But that solitary beacon couldn't shine forever, and when he was called away to army service, his glow had faded from Un-hee's eyes. She spoke of his letters and his poem, and of the conspiracy that had culminated in his death. She related how Ju-han's father had orchestrated the plot, and she could only guess at what twisted delight he received from arranging the marriage of his son with the daughter of his torment.

Shin-char's death, Un-hee explained, and her subsequent forced engagement and wedding, had left her an empty shell carrying a burden far too heavy for one so young. Her leap from the cliff last night had been an escape from a life she never wanted to have, and in truth, it probably should have ended in death. How she was saved she couldn't tell, but she knew that her single step over the edge had set her on a new path, a path of life.

As Un-hee's narration led right up to her previous step, she realized it had been just as she had imagined: she had related her entire history to this woman as though she were sharing stories with an old friend who already knew the tale. While she spoke, they had passed more fields, now some low buildings, now some forest, and Un-hee had wept at times and laughed at others while Soo-mee's face had mirrored her own. Un-hee felt her soul buoy up higher with every step, and her heart tasted healing as her words carried years of hurt and hate away from it.

By the time she finished, they stood next to the bleached side of the *Ocean Pearl* resting at the dock. Soo-mee held Un-hee by the shoulders and turned her so that the two women faced each other on the bustling wharf. She held Un-hee's hand, looked into her eyes and didn't say a word. Relieved, Un-hee smiled back and knew: she understood.

Together, they walked over to the ticket booth where Soo-mee pulled a pile of crumbled bills from her pocket and paid for a one-way ticket to Busan, first-class berth. They went next door to an open-air seafood restaurant and shared a plate of grilled octopus.

"You have seen enough pain to last you a lifetime, my child," Soo-mee said, looking over the dish covered in tentacles and smeared with spicy red sauce. "I hope you can now start a new life for yourself in a new place. It won't be easy, but I see you carry a strength of character beyond your years."

Un-hee grinned at Soo-mee and nodded her head. "I look forward to being able to do things for myself, sister, to make my own decisions. I'm happy to choose my own way." Then she lowered her eyes and stared at the food for a moment. "But all I ever wanted was to marry Shin-char and be with him forever," she whispered.

"I know, child. I know that. But don't let your love or your heart live only in the past. What happened was tragic and unfair, but you know what? It can never be changed. So don't let your precious effort be wasted trying to. Carry what you have known within you, don't ever forget those lessons learned in struggle. They will continue to teach you. Concentrate on the present and give your best to those around you, especially your children. They are the ones that carry hope for a better future."

"I doubt I'll ever have kids now. I promise I will never be bound to any man as long as I live."

Soo-mee smiled and winked at her. "You say that now, and I don't doubt you're sincere, but you may be confronted with a helpless, crying baby sooner than you think."

Just as Un-hee opened her mouth in protest, the boat's horn blasted a shrill call echoing throughout the harbour. She leapt from the table and hurried behind Soo-mee through the crowds, past some fish stalls and vegetable vendors, and out to the long dock.

A short man with a wide face stood next to the ship and shouted for all remaining passengers to get on board immediately. His sweaty fingers checked Un-hee's ticket and waved her on. Soo-mee hugged her farewell, and as she held her tight, she thrust a canvas sack into Un-hee's pocket and shoved her up the gangplank. Un-hee scrambled up the stairs and onto the boat as it slid away from its cement mooring. Turning, she looked into Soo-mee's shining eyes glistening like black pearls set in the bark of a grizzled oak tree.

"Thank you sister, for all you've done," shouted Un-hee above the gurgling engines.

"Go, child," Soo-mee called back, waving her hands forward. "With all the love your heart could possibly hold and more." Her sparkling eyes winked again and Un-hee knew wherever this woman went, her secret would live with her and ultimately be buried in her aged chest, never known but never forgotten.

The ship cleared the harbour's cradle and the engines rumbled underneath, sending a white froth of water churning behind. Un-hee moved along the railing, keeping her soaked eyes steady on Soo-mee at the end of the dock. She reached the stern and watched unblinking until she could see her no more.

fifteen

Ju-han could feel the Colonel's eyes on his back while he followed the path of volcanic slabs around to the side of the hotel. As soon as he stepped out of sight into the cool shade of the trees, he felt relieved. Here, along the hotel's western side, tall pines clothed the hill that sloped down to the stream at the bottom. On the valley floor ran mountain water, swiftly coursing towards its plunge over the waterfall into the salty waves. Ju-han stepped along the slices of stone and looked for a quiet space between the trees. A wind began to sigh through the branches bringing fresh sea air to mingle with the forest's foliage.

Something has changed, Ju-han decided. Maybe it was his father's instructions that poisoned his thoughts towards the Colonel, though clearly Cho himself now sifted for information that didn't belong to him. Either way, Ju-han mistrusted the man, and felt uneasy telling the Colonel anything since his eager tone had betrayed him.

Ju-han reached a bench of stone in a tiny clearing pushed back from the path. On this he lay, looking up into the branches above while the cool rock under him spread shivers down his neck and shoulders. Here, vines and leaves hid from the yellow heat as the wind moved in a cooling rhythm between the trunks of the trees. Ju-han closed his eyes and listened to the breeze twisting over his face and coiling around his ears.

The soul of the forest was still beneath the mighty wood that shaped a green ceiling far above, greeting one other with emerald arms outstretched at their loftiest heights.

Ju-han listened to the wind and felt a peace creep over him for the first time in as long as he could remember. Breathing deeply, he allowed it to swallow him from the inside as his thoughts wandered back to Un-hee. Melancholy and shame spread in his chest, and he knew he had lost that which he had taken by force. Yet in losing her, he still struggled to let go of control. He thirsted after it, even though he knew his fingers were empty, and strangled nothing but his own will.

He swung his feet to the ground and sat up. The hotel's profile now stood like a lumpy black canvas in front of him, the rim of the turret frowning from high above. From this vantage point, Ju-han could glimpse the rear grounds over some hedges, and spy the front lawn through gaps in the forest. As he watched the front, suddenly he saw an army officer appear from behind the corner and stop. The man glanced back towards the front entrance area, gave some hand signals, and continued his approach towards the rear of the hotel. The ivy-choked screen in front of Ju-han framed the officer's face and shoulders for an instant: General Jin.

Immediately, Ju-han crouched and scurried as quietly as he could down the sloping hill behind him. The General was walking briskly, and the clicking from his shoes on the slabs of lava grew.

197

Ju-han scrambled as far as he dared and stopped behind a thick pine that wore an ivy leaf skirt. Behind this cover, he lay prostate and watched as the General's hat bobbed stiffly through the foliage. Then it slowed and stopped, almost directly in front of Ju-han.

The air under the emerald roof now hung stagnant; every leaf held its breath. The hat moved towards the trees so that Jin's face was visible through the coiled vines in front of Ju-han's eyes. The General paused as he looked into the forest; then turned and sat down on the seat of stone Ju-han had abandoned only moments ago. A minute of silence trembled by as the sticks and rocks beneath the forest's carpet dug into Ju-han's forearms. But he wouldn't move, not daring to budge a single cell for fear of discovery.

Another man was suddenly visible seated next to Jin. Ju-han couldn't make anything out but the bald dome of the man's head, covered by wisps of hair pulled over from the side. However, when he spoke, the voice was familiar.

"I just met with him," the man lisped.

"And?" Jin's sandpaper voice shot back.

"He said nothing you haven't heard. I doubt he had anything to do with it at all."

"I care nothing for your thoughts. Tell me what was said and I'll judge whether I've heard it before or not," the General rasped in reply.

"Yes, sir. This is difficult for me as you know." The Colonel mumbled some more words that didn't reach Ju-han's ears.

"I understand well, Colonel, but this is my investigation carrying my responsibility. And as I've already explained to you, this is also a matter of honour to all Koreans. It's bigger than a premature death, and it's more far-reaching than the punishment of one murderer. By aiding me, you are fulfilling not only your military duty, but your civic responsibility as well."

Ju-han heard the Colonel cough and clear his throat. "I approached him and he told me Un-hee was feared dead. I feigned surprise and he continued by saying the hanbok was found but nothing else. He did seem very calm about the whole situation, just as you said he would be. But he also mentioned that he thinks she's still alive, though."

"Really? He said that?" Ju-han saw Jin remove his cap and rub his face and eyes.

"Yeah, it threw me off, made me wonder."

Ju-han's neck began to ache as he held it kinked in an awkward pose in order to see both men through a postcard gap in the leaves. Knives now cut into his elbows and still he would not move. He tried to judge the distance separating him from the men, and figured he could take four steps and touch either enemy. He had no choice: he would lie as a breathing statue until they left.

"The murderous villain. He's lying to keep you and everyone else off his trail. He knew she was dead before he ever threw her off that cliff," breathed Jin into his hands.

"How could you possibly know that?" came the Colonel's reply.

"That doesn't concern you," Jin snapped back, rattling the sandbox caught in his throat. "Continue the conversation."

A pause separated the men before the Colonel proceeded. "He also gave me the same reason for the scars as he gave you. I guess that part must be true."

"Hardly, he just knows how to tell the same lies to everyone. It's obvious his poor bride made those scratches in her death struggle. What happened next?"

"Well, I told him about seeing Un-hee just before he came in looking for her. He was very interested in that part. It stunned him, I think."

"You didn't tell him everything, did you?" questioned the General.

"No, I told him she didn't speak, just like you said I should. He was very interested in what she was wearing."

"What did he say?"

"He asked to describe her dress, and when I told him it was her wedding hanbok, he went silent for a while."

"I knew it! I always knew it, right from the beginning! That murderous snake!" Jin couldn't muzzle a snarl from escaping his clenched teeth. Ju-han held his breath and waited for more.

"And then he said that he has new enemies now."

"Really? And…" the General's scratching tone hung between the trees.

"And when I asked who, he paused and said himself, that he is his own enemy. He blames himself repeatedly for Un-hee's tragic death."

Jin was slow to respond. When he did, a low growl crawled out of his throat: "You fool. You sewed his lips together by pressing him. He might have confided everything to you, all his thoughts, and maybe even a confession. But now," he snorted, "now the truth remains veiled because he no longer trusts you." After another pause, Ju-han heard a sigh. "I curse your foolishness." The General continued in a grating rumble Ju-han could barely understand. "With your prodding, you dried up the only stream that flows directly from the source of death."

Another pause.

"Did he mention anything else?"

"No. I assured him he can lean on me for support if he felt need, and then he left."

Ju-han was startled as he heard a harsh laugh flee Jin's lips.

"Lean on you?" the General croaked. "You splintered crutch that wounds the hand reaching for help? I came to you for help. I needed you to coax a confession from him, but you succeeded only in shutting him tighter. Now I'm forced to bring him into custody with no concrete evidence and no statement. Your stupidity has cost me, Colonel. You've made my job much more difficult than it should have been."

Another pause crept by.

"Where is he now?"

Ju-han couldn't understand the Colonel's sullen whisper.

"Well, where did he go when he left you?"

"He walked over to this side of the hotel and disappeared around the corner."

"You didn't follow him?"

Though Ju-han couldn't see the General's face clearly, he was certain hot blood was rising to its grainy surface.

"Of course not. He would have seen me and then what could I've said? Besides, I figured your men were everywhere. They should have been able to keep him in sight."

"I've been on the front lawn for over half an hour and he never came around that way. So he had two choices: into the hotel through that side door or…"

Ju-han heard the General's shoes scrape gravel as he spun around on the bench. Ju-han sunk deeper into the leaves and vines covering him as he watched the General's eyes roam slowly through the forest reaches. All lay still as the hunter sought his prey, every sense wound tight to snare the other's tune. Ju-han's heart shook inside his chest, and he was sure they would be able to hear it as he tried to remain as still as ice. Drops of sweat curled down from his brow, stinging his eyes and dripping from the end of his nose. The forest's mantle seemed to tighten even more now and leaked no breath of wind through the stiff trees. Ju-han saw nothing but the General's black pearls, floating on mounds of snow and scanning along the forest floor for any movement, however slight. His eyes looked dead into Ju-han's breathless shell, but they passed over without lingering, leaving Ju-han to fill his lungs again, when he was able.

As Jin's gaze finished sweeping through the forest's breadth, he leaned over to the Colonel and spoke into his ear. Ju-han could hear nothing of what was said but as the General elaborated, Ju-han watched the Colonel's eyes slide back and forth between the trees. Suddenly, General Jin left the Colonel, walked up to the hotel, and entered through the side door. Cho remained standing behind the bench, arms folded across his chest and staring into the still, silent heart of the forest.

Ju-han knew his noose had just tightened. He had witnessed the groundwork of an obsessed investigator and the directives for his immediate capture; he had stepped within the gladiator's circle and escape hatches were closing all around him. The General would check with staff inside and soon discover he had not gone through the hotel. He would return to Colonel Cho who was standing guard, and together they would begin a full search of the forest with the help of every available soldier. The hounds would be loosed and the fox had nowhere to run. And the most tragic, Ju-han thought, was not that the enemy chased him, but that a friend had led him. He decided to use the only chance he had left.

"You remember the song, don't you?"

The Colonel stepped back in surprise, and his arms dropped to his sides. "Ju-han, is that you?" he lisped, eyes wide, searching through the forest.

Ju-han stayed hidden among the leaves. "You must remember the song, Colonel."

"What are you talking about?"

"The soft melody sung by the bird just before I shot that N.K. sniper who had you dead within his scope."

The Colonel stood unflinching for a moment before he spoke again. "Ju-han, I don't know what you just heard but…"

"All I needed to hear," Ju-han replied, pulling himself to his knees. He could see the Colonel twisting on the spot, shading his eyes while trying to peek through the foliage in the direction of the voice. "The sound of a blade through my back."

"No, you don't understand. I had no choice. If you knew what kind of pressure…"

"Stop! I've no time for this. You can gather up the rags of your dignity by letting me go right now. If you see any worth in the life I preserved years ago, return the favour in kind today. If I am guilty, let them catch me; but if I am innocent, then give me my chance at freedom."

Ju-han was standing now, his dry eyes and glistening face visible beside a cluster of vines. He stared up at the Colonel across a chasm of rock and tangled ivy while the Colonel's square glasses looked down at him in silent pity. His lips narrowed and his arms hung limp at his sides.

"Go, my son, quickly," he whispered. "I never saw you."

Ju-han turned to flee into the forest, but his feet remained fixed in the pine needles. His gaze swung slowly back to the Colonel again. "What did she say to you at the buffet table?"

The Colonel opened his mouth deny any knowledge of what he was talking about when Ju-han's eyes arrested his words halfway up his throat.

"I'll never forget it, Ju-han," he answered, hanging his head. "Her words will haunt me for as long as I live." He paused and covered his face with his hands. "It was mainly because of what she said to me last night that I agreed to help the General in his investigation of you. She stood on the opposite side of the table, about as far apart as we are now, and she looked at me through eyes that no longer saw. It was like looking into the pale face of death: there was no life, no fear, no love. And her voice," the Colonel shuddered involuntarily. "Her voice seemed to come from the bottom of the sea. It said:

'I jumped for freedom, though I bore no chains,
He killed his bride, though he bears no stain.'"

Ju-han stood rooted in the middle of the forest staring into the Colonel's eyes.

Cho spoke again. "I haven't slept since I heard those words, and I let you leave now only to free myself from the debt of life I owe you from years past. Now go! I wash my hands of you!"

When Ju-han sprung to life, the Colonel yelled after him, "Head towards the ocean and skirt around. The road is swarming with soldiers."

Ju-han paused and looked back at the Colonel's worried brow. Without a word, he swung about and started racing through the woods towards the sea.

Ju-han sacrificed caution for speed for he knew precious seconds had slipped away between him and the Colonel. He ducked under branches and leapt over fallen logs as the forest bled by him, brown and green. Grasping cobwebs ensnared him, and he repeatedly wiped them from his face with his fingers. Soon, his hands and arms were streaming with blood from the branches reaching out their barbs and assaulting him as he fled past. He slowed his pace only when he could no longer see the black walls of the hotel spying through the trees behind him.

He continued down the sloping shoulder of the forest. The pines stretched their boughs as arms and roots as toes towards the sun and stream filling the bottom of the valley. Ju-han found it easier to slip with the grain down the hill than fight each crossing step. His clothes already hung in ribbons from the flight he had made away from the stone seat and the hollow man, and he had no desire to struggle any more than necessary.

As he sliced between the trees, a shadow of doubt spread over Ju-han's brain. What if the Colonel had actually lied to him, he thought, and had betrayed him to the General again? Suppose he told the General in which direction he had fled? Perhaps Colonel Cho had actually sent him into a trap, not from one. No trust remained in Ju-han's heart for the Colonel, but he decided to carry on for he had no alternatives.

Then he remembered the lava tube by the ocean. Maybe I can reach the cave without being seen, he thought, and hide there until nightfall. Though the memory of the dark tunnel still made him shudder, he far preferred it to imprisonment or death under Jin's command.

Farther down the hill, the vines strangling the trunks of the trees grew thicker, and some had even grown so large as to embed themselves into the bark. They swung low and stretched like immense snakes from trunk to trunk, harnessing the trees together. Ju-han hurdled some and crouch under others, trying to avoid being hung by the drooping parasites.

He was bending low under yet another vine when he stumbled onto a stone path. First he looked up the trail, then down, recognizing it as the very path he had taken with the clerk down to the waterfall so long ago. Was it only last night? He remembered the rage that had boiled within him as he had slipped down the blurry trail, and the ocean of tears below that had filled his wounds with salt.

Since then, the ensuing investigation and his imminent capture and imprisonment had occupied his mind so thoroughly that thinking about Un-hee now made his soul thirst for her. Her words to the

Colonel from beyond death's grip chilled his skin, and made him realize that his innocence now meant very little, even to him. Though he hadn't physically pushed her to her death, he knew he had killed her inside before she ever reached that cliff. As she had lain on the bed under his sin-stained hands, she had pleaded for her life, but because he believed she owed herself to him, he had violated her.

Standing in the middle of the forest path under the melting sun, Ju-han clenched his fists and knew there was nothing he wouldn't give to take back his drunken stupor from that drenched, ill-fated night. He closed his eyes and longed to see Un-hee again, her dark, silky hair, radiant smile and soft eyes. How beautiful it would be just to hold her once more, as a wife, as a woman.

To love her for who she is.

To know her like Shin-char had.

To see her radiance next to that fountain while the storm swirled around in the darkness outside. His iron clutch had driven her away, crushed her beyond the threshold of death, and had now turned on his own neck as the net thrown by General Jin drew tighter around him.

Jin! The night vanished, the rain cleared and the sun tossed a dappled pattern of light through the trees. Ju-han opened his eyes and saw the trail again, the most direct route to the sanctuary he sought, but also the one carrying the most danger of discovery. With his torn clothes hanging from him, shredded by the forest's fingers, he weighed his next step.

Suddenly, two black helmets bobbed up the trail from around the corner. Ju-han crouched low and leapt off the path into the choking foliage on the other side. He just had time to crawl behind a moss-wrapped boulder before he heard the clap of boots against stone pass by. When the dead rhythm had faded into the upper reaches of the woods, he turned around and slid to his stomach, peering out at the trail from behind the rock. Sweat curled over his cheeks and onto his neck. The forest was silent, as was the ribbon of path winding up its face.

While Ju-han watched, he tried to decide whether risking the path was even possible. His answer came seconds later as the thudding of boots approached once more, this time falling down on him from above. The sound grew until green uniforms pounded past Ju-han's eyes and fell away through the forest towards the ocean.

When he thought it safe, he turned and crept away from the path, abandoning all direct routes and invisible hopes. He would have to scurry among the undergrowth like an animal until night's murky blanket laid a cover for his freedom. He crawled over thick roots, and beds of ivy and moss carpeting the forest floor. The wind had begun to stir again as far above him, the pines threw back their lofty heads and relished the growing breeze. The trees around Ju-han groaned as their backs bent unwillingly beneath the ocean's breath.

Ju-han crept along through the forest and might have even remained unseen until nightfall if it weren't for the next set of sentinels to patrol up the waterfall path. While lunging off the trail to avoid being seen, Ju-han had brushed his sleeve against a vine, and a green spike had pierced his shirt and held fast to a shred of blue fabric. The soldier had spotted this hanging flag of indigo and the radio link between him and General Jin was soon chattering furiously of Ju-han's ruin.

With arms carved by wooden fingers, Ju-han crawled quietly, searching for a thicket in which to nestle until the sea should quench the last flames of the dying sun. Though he crept away from them, he couldn't have known that troops were massing on the trail behind him and along the perimeter of the hotel lawn above on his left. The noose was tightening further and waited for Jin's direction; he had insisted he lead the foremost soldiers to Ju-han's capture. His voice barked commands through several radios, positioning his wolves to corner the hunted rabbit between a hundred rifles and the sea.

Through the trees, Ju-han could spy again the cool, azure face of the ocean. He reached the brink of the forest where pines held the edge of the rock between their toes and stood watch over the water below. From this height, he could already see the cave's oval staring like a black eye at the waves forever rolling towards it but never arriving.

Something puzzled Ju-han as he looked down at the shore: there wasn't a soldier anywhere. The steps beside the waterfall were deserted, as was the entire rocky coast. To find a higher vantage point, he stood cautiously and started walking along the hem of the forest, staying back from the unclear separation of earth and air to his right. Vegetation hung over the lip of the cliff so that one foot on solid ground could easily neighbour a step that would lead to a swift death among the boulders below.

He had walked for some time, and the cliff was bending higher when he heard a noise behind him to the left, as though a branch had snapped. Ju-han crouched and looked around. He heard nothing more, but saw a figure pass through the trees farther up the hill; a dark shadow that disappeared as fast as it had moved.

Ju-han blinked into the forest while his heart rattled within his caged ribs. Clawing at the earth with his hands, he leapt to his feet and fled from the ghostly forms pursuing him. He tore up the edge of the cliff, an unseen enemy on one side and a plunge of finality on the other while his eyes shone wild with fear. He dodged trees and stumbled over roots, a desperate desire to live flaring within him.

As he darted along the cliff, a pine wearing a leafy skirt appeared abruptly before him. Rounding it, Ju-han's foot stepped on the ivy but continued to fall through, meeting only empty air beneath. His momentum pulled his body along behind his foot and he plunged through the tearing foliage, holding it between clenched fingers in a futile grasp at slowing his fall. He continued through the fringe and burst into daylight, falling faster than ever now.

But he did not fall far. A green-capped tooth of rock held fast to the cliff's face just below the edge and onto it Ju-han fell heavily. His feet hit first, and he collapsed to his knees, smashing his head against the wall of stone. Dazed, he kneeled on the ledge and held his head as blood flowed freely through his fingers and onto his shorts.

As the throbbing subsided slightly, Ju-han pressed his back against the stone and pulled his knees up under his chin, looking around with glassy eyes at his surroundings. A cruel fate eons ago, when lava yet gushed from the island's center, had molded an indent into the cliff wall, and it was through this depression that Ju-han had fallen. He would have plummeted to certain death had the ledge of rock jutting out from the cliff not saved him. What fate had removed with one hand, it provided with the other.

Yet Ju-han couldn't calm his shaking limbs and he continued to draw his breath down into the shallow pan blocking his lungs. He glanced above his perch, where leaves spilled over the cliff's lip, and saw he was not far from the top of the cliff; perhaps he could even reach it if he stretched. Then he remembered what hunted him up there and he was not so eager to try. He looked at his ledge and realized it was hardly wide enough for his legs to stretch out straight without hanging over the side. And five people would have had trouble sitting across its breadth. Saved by a car's hood, he marveled.

Peering between his knees, he saw the sapphire sea far below crushing lines of cotton into boulders and sending their thunder surging up the bluff into his ears. Ju-han felt as though he was perched on the peak of an enormous swaying reed in the sky, and he was slowly sliding off; he did not look down again. In front of him, Tiger Island's boxy frame still sat on the horizon, and by staring next to it, at the unmoving line between water and air, Ju-han was able to quiet his body and pull breath down to the floor of his lungs. He sat cross-legged on his crag and marveled at his luck. Perhaps this was the best place to be at the moment, while the forest above him crawled with treacherous shadows.

Within a minute, he heard a hushed voice whispering above. "Last I saw, he was running this way along the edge."

"I'm sure I saw him run past that tree over there," a nasal tone returned.

"He might be hiding in the undergrowth around here. Search the entire area and seal it off higher up," ordered a deep growl.

Ju-han heard more crackling of branches mixed with the clanking of rifles against metal. He held his breath and melted against the rock behind him.

Suddenly, a wheezing throat pleading for breath approached from higher above. When it spoke, it sounded like gravel being poured into water. "Did you find him yet?"

"No, sir, General Jin. But we will soon. He was last seen in this area and the entire perimeter is sealed off," replied a low rumble.

"You don't have him? You have over 50 men in a secure area and you can't locate one unarmed civilian?"

"I'm sorry, sir. We'll have him soon."

"Where was he last seen?"

Ju-han looked up at the spot from where he had fallen and was horrified to see that the very tree he had dodged just before plunging was partially visible from his perch. He heard the two men continue to murmur to each other as they walked in the direction of the tree. Beside it, Ju-han could now make out a black helmet nodding towards General Jin's hat. The two turned and twisted, and often nodded at each other as Ju-han's breath again only fed the roof of his lungs, and his skin sparkled with dew.

But they came no nearer the edge, and soon disappeared back into the forest. Ju-han exhaled what little air he had trapped within him, and stiffened when he heard the familiar voices again.

"I'm sorry, sir. I can't understand how we haven't located him yet," the deep voice droned. As an afterthought, it added, "Perhaps he fell from the cliff."

General Jin's dry voice slowly scratched an answer. "Yes, you could be right. Perhaps he fell."

To Ju-han, it sounded like the General was smiling as he spoke of the possibility. Then he heard rustling in the bushes above him. His muscles tightened and he pressed closer against the rock.

"I can't see anything down there, but I think I'll send the boats around for a quick look anyway," said Jin. "Hey, what is that patch of green just below us here?"

The rumbling voice answered, "I don't see anything."

"Of course you don't," snapped Jin, and Ju-han heard him stomp away. He thought perhaps the General had left to make a call for the boats, and he had even begun to wonder how he would hide from the navy's probing eyes when he saw Jin's hat and wooden face looking down at him from beside the tree.

"Well hello, Ju-han. We've been looking for you."

Ju-han watched the General's thin face break into a smile. "And here I am," he answered.

"And there you are. Looks like you hurt yourself a bit on the way down. Are you all right?"

Ju-han watched Jin's narrowed eyes in silence.

"What a clever hiding spot you found there," the General continued. "Too bad it wasn't quite good enough." His sandpaper voice gritted as it seeped out from between his smiling teeth and lips.

"I didn't do it, Jin. I never killed her."

"Oh, don't waste your breath! I'm not the one you have to convince. Surely the judge will be itching to hear every word you have to say. My duty is complete just by bringing you in; although I have to give you credit for being slyer than most, even though you did have help."

Ju-han stared back in sullen defiance.

"But not to worry. That weak character will be dealt with, now that he has outlived his usefulness. The army will be better off without him, but I'm not sure he will enjoy his retirement quite as much as he'd hoped." The General's laugh scraped against the walls of his throat. "From what you heard, is there anything you'd like to change about your statement from last night?"

Ju-han continued his restraint, despising the General's satisfied grin.

"Oh, silence is a very powerful tool too. It's worked for your dad for many years but his time will finally come too. Especially now that we have you, I'm sure he'll cooperate."

"What do you have against my father?" Ju-han tensed. He still wouldn't believe what Un-hee had said was true, but he felt a need to know why the General had hunted his father for so long.

Jin dropped his jaw in mock astonishment. "He's kept it from his own son? Unbelievable! I'm sorry to have to tell you this, Ju-han, but your father is a traitor to his nation. He collaborated with the Japanese during the occupation. He betrayed the Korean people to the enemy and was handsomely rewarded for his actions. Though we still haven't uncovered the extent of his treacherous deeds, we do know he helped choose the women that were taken by the

Japanese military to be used as sex slaves. He sold our women to the worst abuse and death imaginable, and received filthy wealth for it." The General's voice shook with emotion. "Your father is a vile man, Ju-han, and we're finally going to be able to bring him to justice."

"You're lying," whispered Ju-han.

"I have a whole pile of evidence in my office that I can go through with you, if you care to see for yourself. But maybe this will convince you: Ju-han, have you ever wondered why your bride hated you so much?"

Ju-han sat stunned by the question, and didn't respond a word.

"Your father had her mother sent to the Japanese rape camps. She died under the torment of those evil men. Un-hee lost her mother when she was only seven years old, but she never stopped searching for her. Through her efforts, last year she discovered your father was behind it all, that he had sold her mother and so many others into the darkest of all deaths. She came to us with the information because her own father refused to believe her. Her own father, can you believe that? And do you have any idea why? Because she was betrothed to you, to be married in the summer. He insisted she marry you because you came from a wealthy family, wealth gained from the lives and tortures of young, innocent women like Un-hee's mother. They're both dead today because of you, because of your father, and because of the Japanese."

Ju-han growled back through gritted teeth. "You lie! You lie because that's the only language you know. My father is an honourable man in his community, and he was a valiant soldier in the Korean army. He would never do anything like that!" He jumped to his feet on the small ledge as rage burned through his body.

Instantly, hands grasped his arms and shoulders from above, and started hauling him up the cliff. He writhed and fought with his elbows while sinking his teeth into any hands near his mouth. They released him after he had bit several of them and he fell back heavily onto the ledge. Shaken, he opened his eyes to see four rifles staring down at him.

"Ju-han, stop resisting and give in. We have you now; it's all over. Where are you going to go?"

Ju-han sat up and stared at the General. "I could jump, Jin. Then you'd have nothing!"

"Believe me, that would be a favour to us all. But you could never jump. You don't have the courage."

And he knew the General was right. Though he faced prison and possibly death under the iron fist of the military courts, Ju-han could never surrender his life to the rocks. He remained crouched beneath the black vultures waiting to bind him.

"Looks like you have two choices," Jin rasped again as he removed his revolver from its holster. "You can give yourself up and we'll take you away, or you can stay on your ledge and we'll

come down there and take you away." The
General slowly pulled back the hammer and
leveled the black pistol at Ju-han. "What's it going
to be?" he shouted.

A moment trembled past. Then, Jin squeezed
the trigger and fired.

The shot burst on the rock below the ledge.
The blast startled Ju-han, who thought the
General was trying to kill him, and he shuffled
instinctively backward. As the shot's echo
bounced down the cliff to the sea, soldiers above
Ju-han groped for him but he was too low for
them to reach. He was so frightened from the
gunshot, expecting the General to keep firing, that
he didn't look behind to see how close he was to
the other side of his perch. He planted his left
hand on the edge where, under the vegetation, a
fissure separated some loose rock from the
secure shelf of stone. The broken rock crumbled
under Ju-han's weight, and he fell backwards,
collapsing the entire side of the ledge.

"Stop him! Catch him!" the General screamed.

The soldiers stretched their arms in vain as
Ju-han plunged over the side, a large block of
stone hurtling down above him. The horrified
General watched as Ju-han plummeted like an
arrow to the black lava shore below.

A wave had just retreated leaving behind
polished boulders when he struck, and was
instantly crushed by the falling rock from above.

Timo Annala

The afternoon sun glistened in the breaker that washed in to cover him.

sixteen

A gunshot exploded across the water. Startled by the noise, Un-hee turned her attention from the fading harbour to the shore across from the ship. Passengers screamed as they jostled past her to catch a glimpse of the distant cliff face. Un-hee saw some movement high along the bluff near the waterfall where a figure seemed to be perched on the wall, just below the top. Suddenly, some rock plummeted to shore, followed closely by the figure and more rock. The ship was so far away and the person fell so fast that Un-hee could distinguish nothing else. Pain filled the floor of her stomach as the figure hit the rocky shore, followed by the muffled clatter of stones.

More horrified screams broke out among the passengers as new onlookers came running to crowd the railing along the shore side of the boat. Un-hee waded through them and fled to the opposite side, wanting to get as far away from the sickening scene as she could. She swayed her way up towards the bow and began to feel dizzy and sick as a wearying exhaustion swept over her. Descending some steel stairs, she followed a narrow corridor, and eventually found the white door of her berth.

Once inside, she climbed directly into bed. The square window next to her cot looked out at the coastline, and she saw the black face of the Sunrise Hotel slipping by, watching tall and proud from the top of the cliff. The pine trees partially blocked the view, and the hotel could almost have been mistaken for an ancient castle, a stone relic rooted in rock and standing unmoved through centuries of salty waves pounding at its shores. Un-hee closed her eyes and was asleep within minutes.

The sun was dipping its orange chin into the ocean when she awoke. The ball of fire blazed from behind a veil of grey, which carved its edges and sapped its strength. From the porthole beside her, nothing else broke the horizon; she was alone. The sun had watched her climb out of her stone tomb just that morning, and it sunk with her floating away to a strange city. In her entire life, Un-hee had never left Jeju Island, and here she was, bound for an unknown town filled with nameless strangers.

She rolled from bed and the walls of her empty stomach ground against each other. As she stood up, needles stabbed into her left arm reminding her of the wound, and she adjusted her sling beneath it. Leaving her berth, she wandered along the railing outside and watched the waves slide past, their foreheads painted orange before they curled back down into the darkening sea. From one side of the ship to the other, there wasn't a strip of land anywhere. She was free.

She discovered a longer set of stairs climbing to a higher level. These she followed until she stood at the top facing the mouth of a restaurant. Windows along its sides stood open, allowing the sea's breath to flow freely through them while the dying sun fired the glass oil lamps that sat on each table.

Un-hee found herself a quiet corner with a view of the stern and waited for a menu. She remembered the sack Soo-mee had stuffed in her pocket and she pulled it out. Rough cord choked its mouth shut as the bag bulged with its contents. She undid the rope and a clutch of W10,000 bills burst from top, struggling to escape. She gasped and quickly stuffed them back in, drawing the bag shut just as a waiter appeared. She ordered two rolls of kimbap and some cucumber kimchi with a glass of water.

Only after the waiter had left, taking the menu with him, did Un-hee realize a man was watching her from across the restaurant. He sat at a table directly across from her on the opposite side of the boat, and rose when she noticed him. His hair looked like wet tar and stretched in rows straight back from his forehead. Beneath his white shirt, he carried bricks for shoulders, and his smile was a mouthful of snow. Un-hee ignored him and turned back towards the ocean.

Slowly, he strolled over to Un-hee's table and stood in front of it. "Excuse me?" he began in a husky voice.

"Yes?" Un-hee said, pulling her gaze from the water.

"I believe I have something you want," he announced, sounding unsure and yet comfortable at the same time.

"And what would that be?"

"A hand to help you and a heart to love you," he replied, placing his hand on his chest.

Un-hee covered her mouth as soft laughter escaped. "Neither of those do I want or need."

"But your circumstances tell me a different story, dear woman," he countered, nodding at her arm. "Might I just be allowed to share a meal with you. If you still wish to reject me afterwards, I will accept it graciously." He bowed and a chain hung from his neck like liquid gold. He was pulling out a chair for himself when Un-hee stopped him.

"Tell me what you want and I'll tell you if you can stay."

"My name, dear lady, is Han Sun-lee and my only desire is to spend one meal with the most beautiful woman I've seen. After that, I can die full of food and happiness."

"Now I know you're lying," she quipped. "You can sit but I might not stay."

"Thank you, thank you so much," Sun-lee replied, sitting opposite Un-hee.

She continued to stare down at the water while Sun-lee glanced around the restaurant, periodically looking back at her. The silence that grew between them made Sun-lee squirm nervously while Un-hee didn't even notice it.

"I needed to come talk to you. I'm not sure if you understand but it was as though I had no choice, as though I was drawn to you since the first time I saw you. Your face was the face of an angel coming aboard the ship."

Un-hee glanced at him but said nothing and looked back into the blackened waves.

"And was that your mother you left behind?"

Un-hee paused but didn't shift her gaze. "Yes," she replied quietly.

"It's clear you both love each other very much. It's hard to be separated from family. Makes life difficult, always wishing you're somewhere else. And then that horrible shooting took place as we were pulling out. I wanted to rush up and comfort you but…"

Un-hee didn't let him finish. "What do you want from me? I have no idea who you are and now you tell me you've been stalking me since I came aboard. I don't need you near me and I don't want you near me. Why don't you just leave me alone?"

"I'm sorry, I'm so sorry," Sun-lee stammered as he slid the chair back in surprise and stood up. "This was all wrong, I should never have intruded. Please forgive me," he whispered as he left her at the table.

She stared at the white tablecloth and did not watch him leave the restaurant. Her food arrived soon after and she chewed through the rice and vegetable rolls wrapped in seaweed while watching the ship's lights leap from wave to wave. More patrons filled the restaurant as song and liquor were soon flowing freely through the night air.

Un-hee paid for her meal and retreated below deck. The melodies from above followed her through the hallways as she sought to reach her berth without running into Sun-lee again. She entered and closed the door behind her. Inside, the air felt thick and hot, so she eased open her window and smelled the soft breeze as it cautiously peeked into the room. She fell asleep to the lapping of waves.

The morning was old when Un-hee stirred from bed. She relished the delicious feel of rest after finally sleeping away her exhaustion. From her window, she saw misty peaks rising purple from the ocean along the edge of the horizon: Busan's jagged crown was drawing near. She walked over to the sink cradling her arm, and washed her face and neck. Racing from her room, Un-hee was intent on watching her destination grow from the depths of the sea. She had no idea where she would live or what she would do but for the moment, all that mattered was that she had escaped death twice, first a living one, then a watery grave, and her adventures were just beginning.

Un-hee stepped up one flight of stairs and turned to run up the next when she collided with a man on his way down. It was Sun-lee.

"Good morning," he grinned. Then he saw Un-hee clutching her injured arm. "Oh, I'm so sorry. Did I hurt it again just now?"

"It's fine, don't worry about it," she replied, carrying on up the stairs. She could hear Sun-lee's steps following her up.

The sky hung void above as Un-hee leaned over the railing to take in the morning air. She looked down and saw a constant wave folding in a clear sheet from the ship's nose and slicing backed into the sea as white rain. Sun-lee's hands appeared on the rail next to hers, but she ignored them and they remained silent. Un-hee left the railing and walked towards the prow where both sides of the boat met at a point of sharpened steel. Here she saw that the distant mountains had already grown prouder, rising from the endless ocean as their peaks clustered like a forest of tacks beneath a blue blanket sky.

"I only want to be your friend," a voice dribbled from behind her. "I thought I could help you. I know I made a horrible start of it, but I assure you, I only had the best of intentions."

Un-hee turned and saw shrunken shoulders, wind-thrown hair, and dark eyes pleading at the roofs of their cages. She saw a ghost of the man that had confronted her in the restaurant yesterday.

"I hear a difference and I see a difference, but you could be a talented actor rehearsing lines for all I know about you."

"My lady, these are sincere words with lips to match. Let me tell you a little bit about me, and maybe then you will trust me. I'm 32 years old, and the youngest son of a wealthy father. I sometimes handle business for him on Jeju Island. For a while now I've grown tired of living on his money and in his shadow, and when I saw you, a spark lit within my brain. You are to me as light to dark. You came aboard this ship alone, carrying not a single piece of luggage. You took a first-class berth when it's clear you don't have much money, and the money you do have you carry around in a canvas bag stuffed into your pocket. You wear this sling and these clothes that obviously have stories woven into them, and you sleep as though you haven't slept in a week. But most of all, I'm attracted by your self-reliance; you walk with a certainty that spreads like a carpet before you. You are a living riddle to me. All I ask is to get to know you a little better before we dock and then we never have to see each other again." Sun-lee held his hands out with empty palms facing the sky.

"There isn't much to tell, and the little there is I probably won't ever tell anyone. But I can see you're at least trying to be honest now and I respect that. Let's just talk about you and maybe we'll get along. Do you live in Busan?" Un-hee asked as she walked past Sun-lee to a bench sprawling the width of the deck behind him.

He followed and sat down next to her. "Yes, all my life. Have you been there?"

"Never. This is my first time off the island."

"Oh, I'm sure you'll like it. It's much bigger than anything on Jeju. Do you know where you'll be staying?"

"Not exactly, but that doesn't matter. I don't think I'll be staying in Busan long." Un-hee watched some seagulls fly alongside the ship, welcoming it to the mainland. They swirled and cried in joyful harmony, and delighted in the treats passengers threw overboard for them.

"Really? I think you'd like it there. I could even ask my parents to put you up for a while until you get settled in," suggested Sun-lee.

"I thought we were to be strangers after the boat docks?"

"Sure, if that's your wish, that you will have." He paused and squinted his eyes towards the horizon. "Are you ever going to return to Jeju?"

Un-hee looked at him and then back out to sea. "I will never go back there."

"Won't your mother miss you?"

"Yes, I'm sure she will..." she bit her lip. "Terribly. I'll miss her too. But she wanted me to leave, and she knows it's best for me." She looked at him and held his gaze in hers for the first time. She opened her mouth to speak, but then looked down at the steel deck between her feet and said, "I thought we were going to talk about you?"

"Sure," Sun-lee shrugged. "What do you want to know?"

"Well, what business does your father do?"

"He always has his hands dipped in many pies at the same time. I couldn't even begin to explain everything he's involved in because I don't know myself. He likes to keep secrets, always pounds around his office saying, 'Knowledge is power!' and things like that. Right now, I'm running errands for him at the Sunrise Hotel. He's part owner of it, along with two other guys."

"The Sunrise Hotel?" whispered Un-hee, still staring at the deck.

"Yes, have you heard of it?" Sun-lee's eyes were intent on Un-hee's face.

"I might have."

"It's the newest hotel on Jeju. Oh, you should see it. It's grand, like nothing else on the island. It's made of lava stones and built like a castle, right on the edge of a high cliff, and the interior is full of the most beautiful colours and designs you've ever seen." As he spoke, Sun-lee waved his hands in the air to demonstrate. "But my dad didn't really have much to do with it at all, though. His brother manages the hotel, and it was his idea from the beginning. He just needed my dad and this other guy on board for the financial side of it. And then my dad got me involved because he says he's too busy to deal with it. Now that it's finally open, it should really take off."

"Sounds wonderful," emptied Un-hee, watching the growing seacoast. The mountains had pulled alongside the ship, guiding it towards Busan's sheltered harbour.

"It is, but we've already had some trouble. I'm actually on my way back to Busan to tell my dad all about it right now," answered Sun-lee.

"What happened?" asked Un-hee, turning back to him.

"I shouldn't tell you too much but..." he looked at Un-hee while he paused. "On opening night, just two nights ago, there was this massive storm. A guest at the hotel fell to her death from the cliffs in the middle of the storm. It was awful. And what's worse, she was a newlywed bride. Her and her husband had just been married that day. The army came but they still haven't been able to find her body, though they searched all day yesterday. And as if that weren't bad enough, a guy fell from the other side of the cliffs just as our boat was pulling out of the harbour. I still haven't heard what happened there but it can't be good. All of this couldn't have happened at a worse time. We had finally swung our doors open for the first time."

"What about that poor woman?" asked Un-hee. "What do you think happened to her?"

"I don't know. They're saying maybe she was swept out to sea because of the storm, but I don't know, I just don't know." Sun-lee held his head in his hands as he looked down at his black shoes. "I wish none of it had ever happened."

"How do you think that woman fell from cliff?" pressed Un-hee.

"I thought about that and it's very strange. They said there was a section of broken railing and she had walked through it and over the edge in the darkness. But when I was behind the hotel earlier that day, the whole railing looked fine, nothing was broken. So I don't really know what happened. The army did say they found her wedding hanbok down on the rocks by the ocean. But nothing else."

"They found her hanbok?" she echoed.

"Yeah, that's weird too. Why would she be outside, in the middle of the night during a storm, wearing her wedding dress?"

"What did her husband say about it all?"

231

"I'm not sure. He only spoke to the military and they're always pretty tight about the information they pass around."

"He probably knows the most of anyone about what happened to her. They should concentrate on him if they want to learn the truth."

Sun-lee watched as Un-hee's gaze turned back to him after wandering over the mountains. His eyes narrowed. "You know more about this than you're letting on," he said, his voice slow and meaningful.

"What do you mean?" Un-hee looked back out to sea.

"You knew about the Sunrise and what had happened there before I told you, didn't you?" Sun-lee glanced down at sling supporting her left arm. His eyes widened and he stood up. "You're Park Un-hee, aren't you?"

Un-hee looked up at him through stung eyes, and realized she needed to take charge before the situation became uncontrollable. She seized her opportunity. "No, Sun-lee, I'm not. But if you promise never to tell anyone that you met me, I can tell you everything you want to know about her."

"You can?"

"Yes."

"How?"

"First, I want you to promise me. If you can't do that, then I can't tell you anything." Un-hee stared unblinking into his black pupils and held them fast.

"Yes, of course I promise. I will never tell anyone I met you." Neither his voice nor his eyes quavered.

Satisfied, she continued. "My name is Park Soo-mee. Park Un-hee was my sister."

"Oh, I'm so sorry," Sun-lee exhaled, sitting back on the bench in shock.

"She was married to Kim Ju-han two days ago."

"That's right, that's the husband's name."

"He's an evil man and comes from an evil family. My sister was forced to be his bride because it was an arranged marriage. Before they were wed, she told me she would never be able to endure life with such an abusive man. Her only love had been killed in the war just six months ago, and her heart still ached for him. Do you follow me?"

"Yes," breathed Sun-lee.

"Well, they were married in Jeju City and they went to the Sunrise for their honeymoon. I felt so broken for her but I thought, she's strong, she'll make it through. That heavy storm hit and somehow, in the midst of the rain and wind and thunder, she fell from those cliffs. I wanted to see if you knew anymore about it than I did, but I guess you don't. I'm still not sure if it was suicide or murder, but I'm positive it was no accident."

"That's exactly what I was thinking."

"When I heard that she had fallen, I went out to look for her too, but I couldn't find her. That's when I hurt my arm on some rocks."

"So you don't know where she is either?"

"No, I wish I did. I'm sure that snake of a husband knows more than he's told the army."

"If he does, they'll get it out of him. Don't worry about that."

Sun-lee watched as the ship entered a channel guarded on both sides by forested slopes rising steeply from the water. "So what led you onto this boat? Where are you going?"

"Well, Kim Ju-han comes from a wealthy and influential family in Gwanju, and my mother feared for my life too after my sister's death. She decided the best way to protect me was to send me away on this ship, so that I might make a better life for myself somewhere else."

Sun-lee sat back against the bench and breathed deeply. "What about your father?"

Un-hee paused and her eyes swung back to the forested walls climbing from the sea. "He's the one who insisted my sister marry this guy so my mom feared he'd do the same to me."

"That's so tragic. How are you able to carry on with all of this?" Sun-lee's brown eyes had grown wide with concern.

"I'm coping. My mother was a strong woman...and she still is. She taught me to be strong through hard times too."

"How is your arm?" he asked, pointing at her sling. "Is it ok?"

"It's still healing but it should be fine. I just wish I knew what happened to my sister."

"Are you sure she died? Maybe she hit the ocean and was able to survive the fall."

"I'm positive she didn't make it. Nobody could live through a plunge like that."

"I guess you're right. That poor guy yesterday showed us how true that is. How horrible! Two people die on our cliffs in our first weekend."

Un-hee glanced at Sun-lee and then quickly looked away when he turned to her. "I wonder what he was doing there," she mused.

Sun-lee sat up with his hands clasped and his elbows on his knees. "I don't know, but I'm going to find out as soon as I get to my dad's office. It looked like the army had him surrounded and then that single shot was fired. What a terrible way to die. I'm sure it'll be all over the papers today."

"Not likely if the military was involved. Are you sure they were there?" asked Un-hee.

"Positive. I borrowed a crewman's binoculars and watched the whole thing. I could even tell you what the guy was wearing."

"Really? What?"

"Tan shorts and a dark shirt, either black or blue."

Un-hee leaked no emotion as she stared at the ship's railing, but on a screen behind her eyes, her memory replayed her last glimpse of Ju-han in the cave.

"And that shot never hit him," Sun-lee continued. "It burst on the rock below and startled him. That's why he fell."

"Really? They must have wanted him for something."

"Or wanted him dead."

Un-hee stood up and walked over to the railing that leaned towards the blooming mountains. Their roots shone white in the sun as Busan spread her cluster of buildings over their lower slopes. Sun-lee joined her along the empty section of fence. "Sun-lee, I have something to ask you." Un-hee turned once more to face him. "And please don't turn me down."

"What is it? I'll do it."

"Can you do all you can to find out what really happened to my sister? I want to know the true story and have peace about it."

"Sure, I can do that."

"And I'd like a memorial made for her by those cliffs so she'll be remembered properly."

"That shouldn't be a problem."

"Can you also find out what happened to Kim Ju-han? I'd like to have an idea of where he is so I can feel safe."

"Sure, but how will I get all this information to you? I don't know where you'll be. You don't even know where you'll be!"

"Leave your address with me, and I'll write you from where I end up. Then you can send me what you've found."

The deck trembled beneath Un-hee's feet and, as Sun-lee pulled a pen from his pocket, she heard the engines slacken to a rumble. Sun-lee scribbled his address on a piece of paper and passed it to Un-hee while their ship slid by cranes snatching cargo from the docks and loading it onto immense boats sleeping on the water. The many-coloured containers filled the steel bellies of the ships and were piled as high as their bridges in the stern.

Un-hee watched as the *Ocean Pearl* neared the passenger port at the very end of the harbour. Two army trucks sat like black train cars on the dock amid the crush of boats and people and cargo. They hung like lead weights from Un-hee's eyes and fear gripped her heart anew.

Sun-lee clung to the railing next to her and leaned ahead. "We're almost there. Our roads will split from each other very soon. Do you have any better idea of where you will go?"

"No. Nothing," replied Un-hee, her eyes skipping over the waterfront searching for any patrolling soldiers.

"Could I make a suggestion? I think Los Angeles would be perfect for you. It's warm, it's far away, and there's a growing Korean community there that could help you through everything that has happened. A few of my friend's families have immigrated to California and they love it."

Un-hee's heart pumped faster and faster. "I'm not sure if I have enough money to make it there. I've never thought of America but it does sound appealing." She watched the ship's nose slicing directly towards the waiting army trucks. "Sun-lee, thanks for your help. I'll let you know when I settle somewhere. I have to go now."

Un-hee left the railing and scurried through the crowd that had gathered on the deck to watch the ship ease into port. She rushed down the stairs and into the small shop that sat between the bathrooms in the middle of the boat. The woman behind the counter watched in wonder as Un-hee rifled through the clothing rack at the back of the store and emerged with a light shirt and black pants, which she promptly threw on the counter. Grabbing a clutch of bills from her pouch, she paid the curious clerk and left.

Bursting into her room, Un-hee removed her sling, threw it into the wastebasket and slid out of her brown shirt and coarse pants. Next, she threw on her new clothes and pulled her hair back tight to her head, choking it behind into a ponytail. Using the make-up in her first-class berth, she painted herself a new face, and heard the ship's horn blast twice before she stepped into the hallway from her room.

Outside, the gangway bristled with the crowds crushing from the boat. At the head of the line, she saw several soldiers mixing among the passengers as they stepped onto the dock. Un-hee's throat tightened as she shuffled closer, watching the black helmets slicing through the stream of people. She had nearly reached dry land when, to her left, a soldier lifted up his head and spotted her. Shouting for her to stop, he pushed through the crowd and demanded her name and her ticket.

"Lee Soo-mee," replied Un-hee, passing her stub to the soldier. The skin on his face stretched tight around his mouth and his helmet looked too big for his head.

"Where do you live?" demanded the soldier as he lowered his eyes onto hers.

"What does that have to do with my ticket?"

"Don't question the army, woman! Do you live in Jeju or Busan?" The soldier's pupils burrowed into her face as he reached out and grabbed her left forearm.

Un-hee couldn't stifle a wince under the intense pain shooting through her broken arm.

"She lives with me. Please don't talk that way to my wife, and please remove your hand from her arm!" Un-hee felt fingers gently grip her right elbow. She turned and saw Sun-lee standing at her side.

"This woman is your wife?" the soldier asked suspiciously, releasing Un-hee's forearm.

"Yes, and we must be going. Our car is waiting for us. This way, dear," said Sun-lee, pulling Un-hee with him.

"Hold on! Where do you live then?" ordered the soldier as they walked past him.

"Here in Busan." Sun-lee flashed his driver's license in front of the soldier's face. "Have a nice day."

"Thank you… again," breathed Un-hee when they had passed between the army trucks. "I really owe you now. I can tell they were looking for me. Maybe someone had tipped them."

"Possibly. But it might be just cautiousness too. Anyway, here you are and you're a free woman."

Un-hee looked around at the shops, restaurants, boats and people that made this busy seaport swell. She had indeed escaped all that had bound her in Jeju. She had just walked through the last link when she stepped from the boat, and every decision that lay in front of her now was hers alone to make.

"Maybe I will go to L.A.," she said, turning to Sun-lee with a smile. "That sounds like good advice. Do you know where I should go for my ticket?

Sun-lee led her through the twisting lanes that weaved along the perimeter of the harbour. Soon, they stood in front of a man with a shiny face sitting under a sign that read: 'International Ticket Booth'.

"I'll take care of this," assured Sun-lee.

He walked up to the clerk and discussed quietly through the perforated glass separating them. Twice, he turned around and pointed at Un-hee as the clerk smiled a toothy grin towards her. He returned to her with a first-class ticket in his hand.

"I told him you were my sister and that you need to go to Los Angeles to take care of our sick mother. You should have no problem with customs there as long as you mention my friend's family name, Kim, who lives just outside L.A. Show them this address and tell them you'll be staying there." Sun-lee handed everything to her and smiled broadly.

"But how much did this cost? I need to pay you back."

Sunrise Korea

"It wasn't as much as you think, but probably more than you have. But let me do this for you. It's the best investment I think I've ever made. And besides, you'll need every bill you have when you get to America. It could be hard settling in."

"Thank you infinitely, Sun-lee," she gushed, bowing. "You've helped so much."

Sun-lee looked into her eyes and opened his mouth to speak, but no sound came. He looked to the ground and then out at the ships. "Your boat leaves in an hour. It's down at Pier 4," he nodded his head forward, "so you better start walking. I'm due back at my dad's office now so I have to leave this way," he gestured with his thumb behind him.

"I'll write," said Un-hee.

"You better," Sun-lee replied as he walked backwards away from her. "Park Un-hee, you better!" He lit a quick smile, turned, and kept walking.

Un-hee stepped hurriedly along the cement wharf. She had to skirt the many puddles that gathered along the walkway, fed by rivulets of water from the countless seafood stalls bordering both sides of the lane. Wrinkled women with smiling faces squatted on the ground and sliced through every kind of seafood imaginable on their wooden cutting boards while water tanks nearby swam with live eels, fish, squid, lobsters and crabs. Sea life's pungent odour filled Un-hee's nostrils as she rushed along.

Pier 4 stretched out into the harbour behind a blue sign indicating "International Passengers Only Beyond This Point." Un-hee showed her ticket to the attendant who directed her to continue to the end of the pier. Her footsteps slowed as she neared the end and her stomach tightened into a fist of apprehension: at the head of the wharf sprawled the largest ship she'd ever seen. Its three smoke stacks beckoned the sky while round portholes peeked out from many different levels along its white side. A swath of blue splashed the length of it, shouting, "Blue Star Line." The stern was propped open and its gaping mouth invited a long line of cars into its belly while forklifts hissed nearby, whining through their chores as they arranged metal crates for loading into the ship's hold.

Un-hee dodged through the chaos and presented her ticket to the crewman standing before the gangway. He glanced at it and called for another uniformed seaman to join him. Together, they led her up into the ship and gave her a tour of the many luxurious facilities on board the *Orient Star* and, as she followed them, Un-hee thought of the clerks that had walked her and Ju-han through the honeymoon suite. To Un-hee, the vessel was a blur of polished chrome, gleaming marble, bowing crewmembers and smiling faces. Finally, the courteous hosts left her at the round door of her suite in the nose of the ship.

She entered and stood amazed at its size and wealth. Her mind filled with the smell of opulence as her memories struggled to attach all she had known to what now lay before her. The berth was larger than her entire home back on Jeju Island: the king-size bed stretched along the carpeted floor, the sinks glittered like oysters from inside the bathroom, and two portholes blinked at her with eyes of sunshine from opposite ends of the room.

Suddenly, the ship's horn blared through her cabin. She chased the blast through her doorway, down the plush hall, out onto the upper deck, and all the way to the railing watching over the prow and ocean beyond. The ship slid forward as tugboats coaxed it away from its cement neighbour. A cool breeze swept over Un-hee's skin while the vessel eased farther from the harbour's safety, and soon the tugboat escorts fell away, leaving the mighty liner to plow ahead on its own power, eager for the voyage across the Pacific.

Long after the ship had left Busan, Un-hee still clung to the railing and drank in the vastness of the water that surrounded her. She had grown up next to the sea, yet it had never seemed so blue nor so large as it did right now. As she finally turned towards her room, she looked beyond the stern and caught the last view of Korea's mountainous coastline she would ever see. It faded bleak and distant before her eyes, and she loved its hues more now than she ever had.

epilogue

Sumi folded the sheets of script onto her lap. She looked over at Greg with tear-stained cheeks and a wavering smile.

"I know, beautiful. I know," he whispered. He held the back of her head as she hid her face against his neck. The afternoon sun had drifted past, and faded orange rays now lingered on the wall above the bed. Several birds pierced the heat outside with their singing while dusk's insects had begun to join together in stringed harmony.

Sumi stood up and looked out at the green lawn, the sparkling ocean, and the dark outline of Tiger Island surrounded by sea. She turned back to see Greg sitting on the bed amid the papers and pictures that formed her past.

Greg lifted another folded page to her. "There's one more here."

Sumi unfolded the paper carefully, seeing that the edges were brown and skin yellow. Inside, scrawling *hangul* script filled the page so Sumi began the translation:

"June 14, 1954
To the precious Park Un-hee,

I enjoyed finally receiving your letter. In fact, I had started to doubt whether it would ever arrive at all! I have done my best in finding what you seek, but it hasn't been easy. At first, I wasn't able to locate anyone in the army willing to tell me anything, and most of the staff at the hotel still won't say a word about it, even to me. Remember the hotel manager? My uncle? He resigned soon after an inquiry into your death took place. My dad was forced to come down here and hire a new manager.

However, I notice new barriers have been set up around the entire cliff perimeter, and warning signs have sprouted everywhere. I also learned that the clerk who checked you into the hotel, Kwan Jung-lee, left shortly after that stormy night and returned to his family in Seoul. When I get a chance, I will try to track him down and find out if he'll speak about anything.

But the most interesting thing I've found out is some guests claim they've seen a ghost floating over the rear lawn and the cliff edge, especially on stormy nights. It wears a white hanbok and sails on the wind. Sound like someone you know? I have yet to see it for myself but I will keep looking.

I did track down a Colonel Cho who has been removed from the military, and he was willing to say a few things. Actually, he was probably the first one to ever see your ghost, and he said he'd never forget it as long as he lives. He told me the whole story: the night you 'died', he was drinking inside the hotel when you suddenly appeared in front of him. Your hanbok and your hair were dripping wet. Your eyes were open and you looked right at him, but it was as if you no longer saw anything. And then, when you spoke to him, your voice sounded like it was coming from underwater. You said:

I jumped for freedom, though I bore no chains,
He killed his bride, though he bears no stain.

Pretty weird, I thought. Have you ever heard anything like that? I'd be interested to know what all that means. Oh, and remember that man who fell from the cliff the day our boat was leaving the harbour? Maybe you've already found out, but that was Ju-han! The army's story is that he committed suicide while they were trying to rescue him. They were unable to get to him in time and he jumped to his death. But the Colonel told me there was a General Jin who wanted Ju-han tried for your murder. He was the one who fired the shot, and Ju-han fell from fright. And it gets stranger, 'like son, like father'. The good Colonel also said this general was pursuing Ju-han's father too, because of the role he filled in sending Korean women to be sex slaves for the Japanese army. He committed suicide with a pistol as the army's net closed around him. You are very fortunate woman to have escaped that family!

I have pushed for a memorial for you but it's going to have to wait until all the investigations and reports are over. I hope you are doing well in Los Angeles. I'm sure things are very different over there, but you are strong. You will make it. You might even have a husband and a child by now, who knows? Take care, and I will write again when I have more news.

Forever yours,

Han Sun-lee."

Sumi sighed and passed the letter back to Greg. "So many things from my childhood make sense to me now, but all this has opened a thousand new questions." She looked into Greg's eyes and smiled weakly. "Let's go outside, love. I need some air."

As the elevator descended her towering frame, the marble diving woman shone with a new light in Sumi's eyes. The lobby and the far doors opening to the rear grounds spoke ancient whispers to her ears, and she felt as though she moved among the ghosts of many years past. The lawn beyond the glass doors bathed in an orange wash as the sun's crescent sank like a flaming blade into the ocean. The pine trees at the cliff edge swayed their needled arms, beckoning Sumi closer. She slipped her hand in Greg's as they walked over to the trees, the cliff and the plaque.

"This is hallowed ground to us now," Greg said as he leaned over the cliff to watch the gentle rollers licking the rocks below.

"I suppose we can tell Tony why no one has seen the bride's ghost for over a year," mused Sumi, her dream of her mother on the cliff edge passing through her mind. "She was finally able to go home."

"That's right," Greg agreed. "And we can also guess whose namesake you carry: a strong Jeju diving woman with a warm heart who saved your mother's life over on that rocky shore down there."

Sumi smiled at Greg and then turned to the horizon, her eyes twinkling as she watched the last burning sliver of sun drown into the sea. Beneath red clouds, an ocean of black spread to the edge of sight, and on it, a multitude of fishing boats were busy igniting their lamps, dotting the sea like stars in the sky.

Sumi stood beside Greg and looked out over the water. The hot blood that had coursed through a young bride so many years ago, fleeing into the ocean and then over it, had returned to its birthplace. Amid the wind and rumbling surf, Sumi breathed and felt whole. She had arrived.

About the Author

Already a world traveler by 14, Timo Annala has lived and worked in five different countries on four separate continents. He enjoys submersing himself into foreign cultures and emerging with the unique viewpoints and folklore that exist in every corner of our world.

Most recently, Timo spent a year on Jeju Island, where the diversity and richness of the Korean people fueled his thirst for the remarkable and impacted him deeply. The rugged beauty of the island and the turbulent, often tragic, history of Korea impressed a tale upon his soul, which he felt compelled to publish for others to enjoy.

Printed in the United States
76112LV00001B/19

9 781410 709493